Peirene

LINDA STIFT

*TRANSLATED FROM THE
GERMAN BY JAMIE BULLOCH*

Stierhunger

D1152102

AUTHOR

Linda Stift is an Austrian writer. She was born in 1969 and studied Philosophy and German Literature. She lives in Vienna. Her first novel, *Kingpeng*, was published in 2005. She has won numerous awards and was nominated for the prestigious Ingeborg Bachmann Prize in 2009.

TRANSLATOR

Jamie Bulloch is a historian and has worked as a professional translator from German since 2001. His translations include books by Paulus Hochgatterer, Alissa Walser and Timur Vermes. Jamie is the translator of three previous Peirene titles: *Portrait of the Mother as a Young Woman* by Friedrich Christian Delius, *Sea of Ink* by Richard Weihe and *The Mussel Feast* by Birgit Vanderbeke, winner of the 2014 Schlegel-Tieck Prize for Best German Translation. He is also the author of *Karl Renner: Austria*.

MEIKE ZIERVOGEL
PEIRENE PRESS

On the surface this is a clever thriller-cum-horror story of three women and their descent into addiction, crime and madness. And at times it's very funny. But don't be fooled. The book also offers an exploration of the way the mind creates its own realities and – quite often – deludes us into believing that we control what is actually controlling us. Uncanny, indeed.

First published in Great Britain in 2016 by
Peirene Press Ltd
17 Cheverton Road
London N19 3BB
www.peirenepress.com

First published under the German-language title *Stierhunger*

ISBN 978-1-908670-30-4

Designed by Sacha Davison Lunt
Photographic image by Jessica Arneback/Millennium Images, UK
Typeset by Tetragon, London
Printed and bound by T J International, Padstow, Cornwall

The translation of this book is funded by Bundeskanzleramt Österreich.

LINDA STIFT

TRANSLATED FROM THE
GERMAN BY JAMIE BULLOCH

Peirene

The Empress and the Cake

For me

I can't eat as much
as I'd like to vomit.

Max Liebermann, 1933

BOOK ONE

She was inspecting the pink and green custard slices, the glazed tarts and fancy meringues piled high in the window of the patisserie. Her dress touched the floor, with only the toes of her shoes poking out. The dress was black and woollen, and around her shoulders sat a black lace mantilla, whose dipped hem was tucked between her armpits. Not exactly the most appropriate outfit for a warm day in early May. She had no intention, so it appeared, of buying anything; she simply seemed to enjoy gazing at the layers of light and dark chocolate, the white cream toppings and the colourful sugar decorations. Just as I was walking past – I was in a hurry that Friday evening; the supermarket was going to shut in half an hour – the woman turned around, looked me boldly in the eye and dropped her purse. She held her hand in front of her mouth as she giggled. I bent down and picked up the purse. Taking it back, she noticed the scars on my knuckles and raised her plucked eyebrows, which locked into sharp angles. Would you like to share a Gugelhupf? A whole one is too much for me, and they don't sell them by the half here. She spoke in a very genteel way, which was at odds with the ill-mannered stare she had just given me. I said nothing in reply, but accompanied her into the shop. Catching the eye of the girl behind the counter, who was sporting a pink, box-shaped hat fastened to her black bun with hairclips, she told her what she wanted. The shop assistant cut a marbled Gugelhupf into two halves and packaged these in boxes like the one on her head. Three euros each, please, ladies. I paid my share and took the box. I was now in possession of half a Gugelhupf I had no idea what I was going to do with; I'd hardly touched sweet things for years. I tried to say goodbye to the strange woman, annoyed by the pointless purchase I'd been coerced into, but she ignored my attempts to leave. You know, even half a Gugelhupf is too much in the end. My housekeeper and I can't eat it all between us. I'll never be the sort of person to buy by the slice, touch wood. There's something dreadfully sad about that and, in any case, the slices are dried out because they cut them early in the morning. My apartment is just around the corner; please do me the honour of joining me for a cup of coffee and some cake. Only for a while, I shan't keep you long. In retrospect I can't say why I followed her, but I did. That was my Saturday ruined. I'd have to go shopping in a supermarket heaving with people. And I really didn't have a clue what I was going to do with half a Gugelhupf after stuffing myself with cake at this woman's place. Even contemplating what might happen with my share was giving me a headache. I was annoyed at having got myself into this situation and displeased that now I was obliged to visit a stranger's apartment. The best thing would have been to leave the cake right there; maybe somebody would be happy to find it. But the thing would probably end up in the bin. I mean, who takes abandoned cakes home with them? While she muttered away to herself I tried to guess the woman's age. Her voice was very soft. You had to concentrate hard when listening to her. The skin on her face was brown and weather-beaten, like that of people who do a lot of hiking or sunbathing, and pronounced wrinkles were etched around her eyes and the corners of her mouth. Despite this she looked young, almost elastic, perhaps because of her upright posture, which emphasized her tall, slim figure. Her dark hair was plaited into an intricate coiffure. We turned into a narrow side street, only a few minutes away from my flat. She unlocked the front entrance to an old Viennese apartment block and we climbed the stairs to the third floor. I concealed my breathlessness as best I could. Ever since I'd been living on the ground floor I'd found going up stairs hard work. When we entered her apartment a dog with scraggly fur leaped up at the woman, standing on his back legs and hugging her with his front paws. He was an Irish wolfhound, almost as large as a Great Dane, with a rough, grey-brown coat and folded ears. His long, thin legs enhanced his scrawny appearance. He looked just like the picture that forms in my mind whenever the word dog is mentioned without reference to a particular breed. And yet this was an intensively bred variety of sighthound, more than 1,500 years old, which almost died out in the seventeenth century. It only survived by being crossed with other, similarly large dogs, *stabilized*, as it's called in breeding terminology. I knew this from Charlotte, who read endless books about dog breeds, even though she didn't have a dog herself. *Mongrel*, I thought as I looked at him. The woman wrestled with the dog for quite a while, before calling Ida! with a hint of hysteria in her voice. She must have shouted this name thousands of times in the past. A thin, concealed door opened and a fat woman of around sixty shuffled out of a cubbyhole cluttered with furniture. The woman stood by the opening, with ruffled, clumsily tied-up hair. She'd clearly been asleep; she was blinking and her face was crumpled, showing the lined traces of a headrest. She wore the same black dress as the other woman, without the mantilla, but it didn't particularly suit her. It was the wrong cut, the arms too long and too wide, while the material was tight beneath the armpits. Wouldn't believe she's four years younger, would you? What a lovely beauty she was, my little Ida, my kedves Idám, she said, glancing at me. And now? Just look at her! Oh well, none of us is getting any younger. She shook off the dog and gave Ida, who acknowledged these comments with a grimace behind her back, instructions to make coffee and set the table in the drawing room. The dog sniffed at me and tried to thrust his stubby muzzle between my legs, which I nervously pressed together. Realizing he wasn't getting anywhere, he went to lie down in Ida's room. If only you knew the lengths I go to in order to – touch wood – keep my figure! But it's worth it; I can eat what I like without putting on much weight. Madame eat like a sparrow, Ida called out unsolicited from the kitchen.

*

I was often present when they sewed her into her clothes. I would read her Heine poems or tell her about my beautiful Hungary. She could not get enough of the endless plains and mysterious forests, the wild horses and legendary riders. Her clothes had to fit as tightly as possible, and the only way to achieve this was by sewing her up. As undergarments she loved little, close-fitting camisoles. I would gasp for breath when I saw how tightly she had herself laced up. How she would berate her lady-in-waiting if she tied too loosely, and how the lady-in-waiting, now dripping with sweat and panting, would keep tightening the laces until the material started to crackle. Her waist measured no more than fifty centimetres; a man could have put his hands right around it. This was no surprise as she barely ate a thing. To appear even slimmer, she wore none of those voluminous petticoats which bulked out dresses enormously, but long drawers, made of silk in summer and the finest deerskin in winter.

*

The drawing room was stuffed full of carpets, divans, small tables and imitation rococo armchairs, generating an oppressive intimacy that made you feel like an intruder. Dark-red brocade curtains hung in front of the windows. The nest of an alien species. In one corner stood a birdcage in which two light-grey parrots with red tail feathers and white eyes were jabbering away to each other. In another corner was an old television, beside it a video recorder and in front of it a bottle-green TV recliner with footrest and tilt function. The only concessions to the present. The present twenty years ago. Propped up all over the room were grainy photographs from the nineteenth century: boys in sailor suits and pirate costumes; girls in conical ruched dresses; women with top hats or wrapped in Arabic burnouses, surrounded by large hunting dogs or clipped poodles with lion's manes; young men in uniform with sables at the hilt; even a portrait of Emperor Franz Joseph with his obligatory mutton chops, the embodiment of staid bourgeois life; as well as several pictures of the young Empress Elisabeth, including a small copy of the famous painting in which Elisabeth is dressed only in a nightie, her long hair tied in a thick knot in front of her chest. Some rings, the sort that gymnasts use, hung from the door frame between the drawing room and a second room, which was fitted out with similar rugs and furniture. The rings alleviated the sinister atmosphere somewhat. In an unfamiliar apartment my first thought is always how I would change the furnishings, what could be thrown out to make the room look better. Often it's just a little thing upsetting the overall harmony, sticking with fashions that once made sense, or a temporary solution that over the years has blended in with the rest of the room and no longer appears makeshift to its owners. Here, there was nothing to do. The interior, including the gym rings, was perfect in its own way, although terribly depressing. The sooner I got out of this apartment the better. My hostess, who now introduced herself as Frau Hohenembs – she didn't mention a first name – had sat in the only chair with armrests. The housekeeper pushed a trolley into the drawing room and put on the table the portioned cake half – the slices cut thickly – a pot of coffee, three cups and three small plates. The coffee sloshed out of the spout and the cups clattered on their saucers a touch longer than might have been expected, the sound ringing in my ears. The parrots made noises not dissimilar to the clattering; you might even have construed it as laughter. Ida had put on a white doctor's coat over her dress. It was tight across the chest and too short, with the result that her dress showed beneath it and her overly long sleeves protruded from the arms. She folded a napkin twice and laid it on the tablecloth, hiding the coffee stains she had just made, placing on it a framed photo of a woman sitting side-saddle on a horse, her legs covered by a dress, and holding a fan to her face.

She poured the coffee, first Frau Hohenembs, then me, then herself. Her fingernails were bitten to the flesh, something I'd never seen on an elderly woman. Ida took off her housecoat, hung it over the back of the chair she was sitting on and looked at Frau Hohenembs. Only when my hostess had taken a plate and broken off a piece with two pointed fingers did Ida start eating too. She now looked a little fresher than before: her hair had been put up again and her face was no longer marked with lines from the headrest. Her fuller figure meant she had fewer wrinkles than Frau Hohenembs, who definitely fell into the category of thin, if not emaciated. Ida rapidly ate four pieces of cake, one after the other, pouring herself a refill of coffee each time without worrying whether Frau Hohenembs or I had finished ours. Frau Hohenembs only sipped at her coffee, whereas my cup was already empty. Although I didn't like the coffee – it was too bitter for my taste – I had knocked it back in two gulps. I crumbled my Gugelhupf on my plate. If I had cake now I wouldn't be able to eat any dinner; I'd much rather be enjoying some salad or a cheese and tomato sandwich. This wretched cake was unsettling me. What's wrong with you, don't you like it? Frau Hohenembs asked, holding her gnawed piece of cake between thumb and forefinger. I put a large chunk in my mouth. What makes you think that? To change the subject I asked her why there were these pictures of the empress everywhere. She shrugged and gave no reply. I pretended not to have noticed this rudeness and looked around the room with a display of interest. I pointed to the rings that were set fairly high. Do you exercise on those? I said, trying a second time for an answer. Well, I used to, you know, in the past! Sometimes I still swing back and forth a bit, but I'm really too stiff these days. You're very welcome to try them out if you'd like. I can talk you through a few exercises. Ida, lower the rings. No, thanks, I declined, even though I was quite tempted. At school the rings were the only thing I didn't loathe. Better not, I might bring up my coffee, I offered by way of an excuse. In any case, Ida had ignored the instruction, pouring herself more coffee instead. At least take another slice, then, Frau Hohenembs said, offering me the plate after Ida had already put out her hand, which now grasped at thin air. I took a second piece of cake and devoured it in three mouthfuls.

*

As time went on my kedvesem rarely joined in with large family meals. If she ate anything at all, she would usually have the dishes brought up to her private apartments. The emperor sometimes came to see her at breakfast; this was the only meal of the day when she tucked in properly rather than indulging in her peculiar dietary habits. In the early days of her marriage she tried to introduce Bavarian beer at dinner, but her mother-in-law disallowed it, deeming the drink insufficiently smart for the ladies and gentlemen of the court. This, combined with the stuffy formal ceremony of mealtimes, thoroughly ruined her enjoyment of eating together as a family. From that time onwards she consumed beer less frequently, only when she visited the Hofbräuhaus in Munich. Instead she would drink milk from selected goats and Normandy cows, freshly squeezed orange juice and that horrible meat juice. On her beloved maritime voyages there always had to be two goats, which were usually seasick and gave no milk. They would start bucking the moment they came on board and the sailors had to drag them forcibly by their tethers across the deck. Many a lady-in-waiting suffered in similar fashion; my édes lelkem alone had the sea legs of an old captain, and she even had herself strapped to a mast in a storm – the more tempestuous the better as far as she was concerned.

*

I placed the cake on the kitchen table. The coffee had made me jittery. Coffee always unsettles me. After an initial hesitation I'd eaten the first slice of cake with some relish, the second was forced on me against my will by Frau Hohenembs, the third I helped myself to without invitation because it was irrelevant by now. I'd forgotten that it was always relevant; no matter how much you ate you didn't have to keep eating just because it was irrelevant, you could always stop. I gazed at this thing with its light and dark marbled ribbons, like narrow flags blowing in the wind. With its round folds, it had the appearance of a bulging fan. In places the icing sugar on the ridges and in the valleys had worked into the crust of the dough and shimmered white. I picked out a knife from the drawer and let it slide slowly through the Gugelhupf. I ate the slice standing up. The soft, slightly crumbly mass spread pleasantly to all corners of my mouth. I could taste cocoa powder and lemon zest, with a hint of vanilla. I cut the next slice slightly thicker. On the third I spread apricot jam, which had stood unopened in the fridge for two years, and the fourth I dipped into a jumbo mug of cold chocolate, which I had made myself. I cut the final piece into two and held a slice in each hand, both thickly buttered, then took alternate bites from them while squatting down to inspect the fridge. I took out everything that was more or less edible and ate it, rapidly and silently. I was abandoned by the day. A faint trance descended onto me like a silk cloth. I went into the bathroom and regurgitated the whole lot. The grotesque face of my abnormality, which had lain dormant within me, resurfaced. It was the first time in fifteen years. I had always known that there was no safety net. But I hadn't suspected that it would arrive so unspectacularly, that it would not be preceded by a disaster such as heartbreak or dismissal or a death. It was as if I'd absent-mindedly taken the wrong path when out for a walk. The silk cloth was pulled away. A visit to an elderly lady had sufficed. On the way home I thought about inviting Charlotte for breakfast the following morning and giving her the rest of the cake. That was unnecessary now; there was no way I could see Charlotte. How could I let her see me? I stood in front of the mirror and looked at my naked belly. There it was again. It had reannounced itself after a long phase of restraint or sleep, while I had painstakingly ignored it. Maybe all that time it had been waiting for this opportunity and was now demanding the attention and control it regarded as an ancient right. I've spent half my life pulling in my stomach. As if that could possibly fool anyone. I heard a banging and crashing in the flat above me, which could only be someone shifting furniture around or jumping up and down. The two pairs of double doors in my room creaked on their hinges. I resisted the urge to calculate my body mass index. I could not resist the scales, however; they showed half a kilo less than the previous evening. I pushed them under the chest of drawers. If I didn't have to look at them everything would sort itself out; a single relapse wasn't enough to send me into free fall. It had been a mistake to buy a set of scales, that was obvious now. At least they weren't digital scales that calculated to the tenth of a gram. In the past I'd frequently get on the scales every few minutes. When my parents were at home I would slip into the bathroom and stand on the scales, very gently, so that nobody could hear the needle racing upwards. Before a meal, after a meal, before having a pee, after having a pee, naked and dressed, so I knew how much to subtract when I weighed myself with my clothes on, which was most of the time. And always very carefully, as if the scales could be cheated by sneaking up on them. Leaning on the edge of the sink and lowering the final half a kilo in slow motion. Making myself as small as possible (and thereby supposedly lighter), crouching. I can't stand on scales normally, as men do – with a firm stride, making the needle wobble around noisily for several seconds. It was sheer torture for me if I weighed half a kilo more than on my previous check half an hour before. And indescribable joy if I weighed less. The mere presence of a set of scales causes me physical discomfort, that's even without standing on them. The large scales you sometimes find at railway stations are particularly unpleasant. They entice me, I slink around them, I even check to see whether I have the right change. But I will never climb on them. A stranger could peer over my shoulder, glimpse my weight and draw their own conclusions. I really wanted an apple to get rid of the stale aftertaste, but I had eaten everything, including the apples. Eating and puking scrapes and scratches away till you're empty, but some residue always remains. An empty vessel with persistent filth sticking to the insides, that was me. How quickly my muscle memory had returned, so horribly familiar. Fifteen years had been swept away. Perhaps I ought to ring Charlotte after all, I thought. But the moment I articulated this possibility, the outcome was a foregone conclusion.

*

From the very beginning she placed her trust in me. She was surrounded by people who were slavishly loyal to her mother-in-law. She impressed on me that I was to listen only to her and not let anyone tap me for information, which a variety of ladies-in-waiting attempted to do from the outset, in subtle and not so subtle ways. But I told them nothing. Édes szeretett lelkem, I was hers and hers alone. As the emperor's mother had a keen dislike of Hungary and Hungarians, she naturally loathed me. The Bohemian ladies-in-waiting at the Viennese court, who prided themselves on speaking French and Italian, but could not master Hungarian, seethed with rage whenever we used my mother tongue in their presence. My lovely mistress! What an enchanting accent she had. My rosy petal! How I missed her when we were apart; I thought about her incessantly. Her pretty face. Her proud demeanour. She was herself like a Hungarian. To me she was all the world.

*

We had gone for a walk by the old racecourse, Frau Hohenembs, Ida, the dog and I. The two of them were wearing the same black clothes as the day before, the dog the same rough greyish-brown coat of fur. I was the only one dressed appropriately for the occasion, in jeans and a T-shirt. Frau Hohenembs hastened along in high spirits, with us in tow as if on an imaginary lead.

The dog ran ahead, came back, ran off again, came back again, panting and with his tongue hanging out, seemingly in anticipation. Probably of a stick being thrown. Ida was wheezing; she was too fat to keep up with this pace. More critically, she had the wrong shoes on, not practical boots like Frau Hohenembs or trainers like me, but pumps with spiky heels that kept sinking into the grass with every step. She was carrying a wicker basket with picnic things; that morning she had called me on the landline at my flat. I had no idea where she'd got the number from – I was ex-directory – and when I quizzed her about this she just laughed and said it wasn't difficult, Frau Hohenembs had her connections. Then, on behalf of Frau Hohenembs, she had invited me for a stroll and a picnic in the Prater. I was about to wriggle out of it with an excuse – a walk on a Saturday afternoon with two elderly ladies was not exactly my idea of a weekend outing – but Ida was so pushy that I was left with no choice. She said Frau Hohenembs would be inconsolable if I declined. In the end, and to my astonishment, I accepted, perhaps to spare me further talk, but maybe I was also glad of the opportunity to leave the scene of my debauchery. I was dead tired. I'd erased all the traces: cleared up, swept, hoovered, mopped, washed crockery, polished all the work surfaces, the sink, the loo. This spanking cleanliness and the smell of detergents were a screaming indictment against me. As was the bulging rubbish bag standing beside the door like a self-satisfied, pot-bellied superego. How would I be able to explain this cleaning frenzy to Charlotte, who was well aware of how seldom I clean? I couldn't have her enter my flat until it showed signs of being lived in again. The evidence of my personal devastation, too, would need time to fade. Swollen lymph glands and a bloodshot right eye. I offered to take the basket from Ida, but she wasn't having it. Neither of them commented on my eye. Frau Hohenembs kept scuttling ahead and we followed on behind. She was looking for a suitable spot for our picnic, but nowhere seemed good enough. We circled the racecourse several times; by now I was wheezing like Ida, but Frau Hohenembs was in inconceivably good shape: her face registered nothing. Her breathing was calm and regular. The exertion was making me sick. To punish myself, I hadn't eaten anything since the night before, and had drunk far too little, so now I felt dizzy. I said I couldn't manage another step without some water and a bite of something to eat. I obstinately remained where I was, the dog howled and Frau Hohenembs looked at me as if we'd never met. Ida, give her some of the broth. Touch wood, it'll help; it's good for everything. Ida dropped the basket, reluctantly undid the leather belt tied around the middle, lifted the lid and took out a green Thermos flask and a silver cup, gilded inside. She half-filled it with a dark liquid by holding the flask up as high above the silver vessel as her short arm would allow and letting a thin trickle dribble into the cup. Her fingernails looked even worse than the last time, edged with dried blood. Without looking at me she offered the cup. It was slightly steaming and I drank down the broth in one gulp. It must have been some sort of thickened beef soup and I fancied that I felt myself instantly regaining strength. More! Frau Hohenembs ordered. Don't be so stingy, and Ida hesitantly poured me another cup, once more filling it just halfway. This time I drank it with small sips and only now did I detect the various flavours. There was an intense taste of beef, carrot and parsley, viscous on the tongue, and I had a slight, not unpleasant feeling of fullness. I could go to sleep now, I thought. Already impatient because of the delay, Frau Hohenembs urged us to move on. We had to circle the racecourse one more time until she finally chose a place, and Ida and I sank into the grass. Frau Hohenembs looked at us both blankly. I'm used to this from Ida; she's overweight and short of breath, but a young woman like you? She took a white damask cloth from the basket, unfolded it sloppily on the grass and, without any apparent system, started piling it with cutlery, plates, cups, dishes and terrines of various sizes with lids – everything made of solid silver – until there was no room for any more. Ida, whose job this should have been, lay stretched out on the ground, wheezing with a rattle in her throat. Her large belly rose and fell too quickly. If only I were in Corfu, she sighed. The tall-legged dog stood perplexed beside her, waiting. I poured some mineral water from a plastic bottle and offered a cup to Frau Hohenembs, which she took with gloved fingers, gave one to Ida, then drank two in succession myself. Frau Hohenembs paced up and down impatiently, commenting that Ida had rested long enough. Ida sat up awkwardly, holding on to the dog for support; it didn't move a muscle. She started unpacking the food and arranging it on the dishes. There were little schnitzels, rice and peas in a ring, rolls of ham, stuffed vine leaves, potato salad, mayonnaise salad, herring salad, shredded pancake, stewed plums and Esterházy cake. Ida poured the soup I'd tasted earlier into two cups, giving one to Frau Hohenembs and keeping one herself; clearly there wasn't any more for me. The dog lay down beside the blanket, gazing longingly with his canine eyes at the dishes. Frau Hohenembs, who by now had walked around our picnic spot several times, finally sat down in the grass and arranged her skirt, lengthening it by buttoning down the hem. She took off her gloves, had Ida undo the buttons on her sleeves, which were then pushed above her elbows, and held her pale forearms in the sun. Around her right wrist she wore a blood-red velvet armband, tied tightly; in the crook of her right arm were greenish patches and dots that looked like needle punctures. She sat up straight, surveying the dishes and comparing them with a handwritten list on laid paper that Ida had handed to her. Ida waited – no, lurked – until Frau Hohenembs finally started eating, then she slurped down her soup before purposefully embarking on one mouthful after another, chewing and swallowing, mechanically and tenaciously, as if called upon to solve a difficult task. Frau Hohenembs sighed at Ida's eating habits. She herself ate slowly and only one or two morsels of each dish, as if she were her own personal taster, but was soon finished with her lunch. I ate only a little, one schnitzel and some rice and peas, none of the salads, which were too fatty for me to keep down. If I'd known that once Frau Hohenembs had finished her lunch, which she signalled with a sweeping gesture of the hand, Ida, her mouth full, would immediately pack away the picnic, plates, dishes and all, while secretly stuffing leftovers, I would have eaten more, or at least put something in my pocket. There was just time for tea out of tiny silver cups and a praline each before this hurried picnic had come to an end. How I would have loved to lie on the grass for a while, enjoy a short doze or stare at the sky, but Frau Hohenembs was relentless. She unbuttoned the hem of her skirt, pulled down her sleeves and held out her arms to Ida so that she could fasten the necessary buttons. Then she rounded up Ida and me and directed us to the fairground in the Prater, talking about a performance somewhere around here that we absolutely had to see. I bought a bottle of cola. With each sip I could feel it corroding the schnitzel in my stomach and to top it all I got heartburn. We wandered around for a while, the big wheel to our left, then to our right, but nowhere could we find any sign that the performance was taking place. According to Frau Hohenembs, a woman missing her bottom half was going to sing Viennese songs. During our odyssey she said breathily – as if by way of an apology – that she was magnetically drawn to the Prater. She couldn't help it; it was at a place like this that she had earned her first and only money: coins that she had caught in her skirt after dancing in front of total strangers, as a child, to tunes that her father had plucked on the zither. She still had these coins; she was fortunate never to have been in such precarious circumstances that she'd had to spend them. She chuckled and then slapped her hand over her mouth – it was probably meant as a joke. Ida said that even if she wanted to she wouldn't be able to spend the coins these days. She'd got them so long ago that they'd been out of circulation for years. I imagined that every few weeks Ida had to polish those coins till they gleamed. Offended, Frau Hohenembs said nothing and pulled at her gloves. Several times we passed the large area where strange creatures made of painted plaster wound their way out of the ground and over it, ossified in their movements, with distorted faces and grotesquely twisted limbs. The backs or bottoms of some of them were formed like seats. Presumably they represented cabaret performers, contortionists, fat men with top hats and tails, grimacing beanpoles wearing trousers that were too short, beneath which their ankles protruded like abnormal swellings, women half-naked or in garish circus leotards. I felt strangely disconcerted by this sight. Almost offended. Perhaps it was the painful body contortions that provoked my disgust, because they recalled some undefined torture, duress and ultimately death. Even Frau Hohenembs groaned when we passed them. These faces again, and she looked away, whereas Ida and I, despite the repugnance the figures induced in us, eyed them longingly, desperate to sit down and relax on their behinds. At every shooting gallery Ida had to ask where the dubious performance was taking place, but nobody had heard of it. We'd prob-ably got the wrong day, or year, for they, the stallholders, were usually the first to find out about things like that. But Frau Hohenembs refused to give up and in the end we not only went to every shooting gallery and every restaurant, but also asked at the ghost train, in the sex museum and at the flying carpet. At the sex museum a midget had handed us a badly printed brochure which contained information about opening times and the *attractions*. Ultimately Frau Hohenembs had to admit that she'd been mistaken and suggested we visit the sex museum instead, which would be both educational and entertaining. She would buy the tickets. As we approached the till we noticed that the midget who'd given us the brochure was aiming a shotgun at us. We stopped; he lowered the gun and grinned. He sat on a bar stool in his tin booth, the door of which stood wide open, and waved us over. He had a hump on his back. Frau Hohenembs smiled at him and said, Three, please, then asked whether she might touch the hump as it brought good luck. The midget consented and pursed his lips. She stepped into his booth and removed her right glove. She rubbed her now bare hand up and down his hump, the red armband shimmering faintly, while he very slowly tore three tickets from a roll and then hesitated before offering them to her – a clear indication that this was quite enough hump-rubbing. She reluctantly took the tickets. By her own admission, Frau Hohenembs rarely had cash on her, so Ida paid. She enquired about a cloakroom and the midget said they didn't have one, but they could leave everything with him, including the dog. Ida put the basket in the booth. What did you do to your eye? he asked casually as he bent down to tie the dog's lead to his bar stool. Ida and Frau Hohenembs gave me a look of keen interest, as if they'd been waiting all this time for me to explain the state of my eye. I simply said, A burst vein, as if it were the most natural thing in the world. The midget nodded and started to stroke the huge canine head, which was now in his lap. He didn't mention my swollen lymph glands, nor my scarred knuckles, for which I was very grateful, as I'd seen from his expression that he'd definitely noticed both of these, and I didn't know how I would be able to account for them without exposing myself to ridicule. Painted on the lead sheeting above the entrance to the sex museum was the image of a woman, naked, with orangey-brown skin and long, wafting hair of an indeterminate colour, somewhere between beige and dishwater. Her legs were too short and too small in relation to her upper body. It looked as if she were shrinking from below, or was this a preliminary stage on the way to the woman without a lower half? An allusion to the midget cashier? If you were being kind, you might also say it was the view from a bird's-eye perspective. But if that had been the intention then it had failed. Perhaps it depicted Alice in Wonderland immediately after she'd taken a sip from the bottle labelled *Drink me* and had started to shrink. And yet Alice's shrinking was rather different; she closed up like a telescope. I'd have preferred to come to this place with Charlotte. We were now standing in a corridor lit by dim lamps; on the walls were pictures evidently by the same artist who'd painted the nude above the entrance. They showed a variety of orgy scenes and were definitive proof that the artist had failed to master perspective. In the first room, just as gloomy as the corridor, a sign said: *The History of Sexuality*. Behind glass hung daguerreotypes from the mid-nineteenth century, the beginnings of erotic pho-tography, gleaming in sepia colours. Girls on their own or in pairs lying on divans, draped with veils or flowers, posing with feather dusters or leaning against trees, wearing happily mischievous expressions, seemingly oblivious to their fat thighs and bellies. This was quite different from the snarling, well-toned models of our era, who offer no more than a frosty smile that is claimed to be seductive. Frau Hohenembs, too, was fascinated by the pictures; she studied each one in detail. Why have these been kept from me for so long? she complained. But in every discount bookshop you can find books full of these sorts of images, filling entire walls of shelves, I said in her direction. She cried theatrically, But back then, back then! Ida! My album of beauty! In fact, where did that get to? These things always mysteriously disappear. Touch wood, you'll get me one of those books first thing on Monday. Not too expensive, mind! Ida muttered something, the only word of which I could make out was *Corfu*, and took a closer look at the photos. She had to be short-sighted, her nose almost pressed up against the glass. Those diplomats must have kept these pictures for their own use, sending you only the clothed ladies, she said, seemingly delighted to have solved the problem. Villains! Frau Hohenembs exclaimed. Villains the lot of them. They always intrigued against me. Always! She fell silent and stared, her mouth agape, at a series of *ethnographic* photographs, showing black women wearing necklaces or naked without any jewellery. Some were painted or ornately scarified, most had their heads shaved; the hair of only a few was braided into little strands, entwined with string or decorated with pearls. Moors, she whispered, female Moors. They're black Africans, you don't say Moors these days, or Negroes, Ida instructed her. Really? Whatever takes your fancy. Are there books with black African women too? she asked me, pausing deliberately before uttering the word *black*. Of course, I said. There are books on everything. But they're called black women. How do you know they're from Africa? Excellent! Capital! Ida, on Monday you're going to go and buy some books with Negro women in them. Ida didn't answer; she was already in the next room. Frau Hohenembs could not tear herself away from the pictures of what probably were black

African women after all, for where would these photos
have been taken if not in Africa, by white ethnologists
under the hazy pretext of the male spirit of research?
The next section exhibited what were purported to be
the first ever sex magazines, from the 1950s to the 1990s.
It was scarcely conceivable that they hadn't existed
before then. As the decades passed the women got thinner and fitter. Whereas in the 50s they had cellulite on
their thighs and powerful upper arms with dimples, and
the beginnings of a tummy (be it small or large), they
slimmed down in the 60s and even more dramatically
in the 70s; in the 80s and 90s they became muscular and
toned, which spoiled the eroticism. Men first made
occasional appearances in the plush setting of the 80s,
standing sheepishly with shining, pumped-up torsos
beside women to whom they offered their stiff members
like gifts, or stuck them straight into their mouths,
vaginas or anuses. Masks ought to have been put on
these men, for their inane expressions were anything
but arousing. A wooden flight of steps led into the next
room, which was devoted to *Perversions*; it looked more
like the showroom of a sex shop. A skinny golden whip
stood on a faux-marble pedestal, and in a cupboard
beside it, were large handcuffs and leg irons, beneath
them a sign saying: *Middle Ages*. A glass case had been
placed in one corner, containing tack, stirrups and spurs,
all thrown together, as if two horses had been unhar-
nessed in a great hurry. In the opposite corner was a
display of latex penises, in various colours as well as

transparent ones, sorted by size as if they were the children of a Protestant pastor, the final and largest one in the row measuring fifty centimetres. I gave the latex penises a thorough examination: some were crafted realistically, others with pronounced veins or covered in warts and tassels. I compared the different bumps and grooves, but it didn't do anything for me. Not my thing, Frau Hohenembs said behind me, brushing my shoulder with her gloved hand. I hadn't heard her coming. She was making for the riding tack and whip, but they didn't seem to please her either. Ida was already in the next room, dedicated to rubber and leather fetishes. Had there been a sign, it ought to have read: *Bizarre*. There were photographs of women from all continents and of almost all ages, laced in the most diverse ways into rubber and leather suits, with zips or cut-outs for the genitals. Some were wearing gas masks or had golf balls between their teeth. Others were strapped together or tied up like packages. There were no men at all. Frau Hohenembs stood by a photograph of a wet, naked woman whose dark, likewise wet hair practically reached down to the floor, and who was tied with coarse twisted rope to a ship's mast. The ship was clearly in a storm, everything blurred and drenched by sheets of rain. Frau Hohenembs's back was straight and stiff; she looked at the picture with intense concentration. I noticed that, apart from the buttons on her hem and sleeves, there were no other buttons or zips to be seen, nor any laces or other fittings such as hooks and eyes, with which you might normally fasten and unfasten clothes. She looked as if she'd been sewn into a case. The picture that Frau Hohenembs was studying so carefully didn't belong in this gallery; it looked far more like a still from a film. The woman's facial expression was not anxious or contorted with pain, but expectant. A female Odysseus resisting the Sirens. In the centre of the room stood a mannequin with a bright-red, screaming mouth, dressed in a black diver's outfit and a diving mask on her head of blonde hair. *Please touch*, it said on a cardboard sign. With two fingers I stroked her thigh and placed my palm on her rubber-covered belly. It wasn't a smooth rubber, but a slightly porous material or foam rubber. I would have preferred it to be smooth; a smooth rubber would have given stronger emphasis to the fetishism. Although it was exciting to put my hand between the mannequin's legs, I found it embarrassing in front of Ida and Frau Hohenembs. The latter was gazing avidly at the photographs again and calling for Ida. Take a good look at this; there'll be books with this in too, she said. Ida strolled down the photo gallery, pulled a small jotter from her ill-fitting dress and made notes.

*

At court they feared the picnics she organized for Gypsies, showmen and all manner of other shady characters. She had such a big heart, my beauty! Especially for the poor and disadvantaged in the world. Whether in the Prater or the Gödöllő Palace, the travelling people were always allowed to sit on the lawns and had to be served by the court attendants as if they were royal guests. For this the court attendants despised my szeretett angyalom, because they were obliged to wait on men, women and children dressed in rags. Each time they would count the silver cutlery and plates because it was plainly obvious to the servants that the Gypsies would try to make off with everything that wasn't nailed down. She, however, would walk with her tall frame between the colourful rows of ragged individuals, sitting either on the grass or on benches that had been put there especially for the occasion. She would stroke children's scratched heads, let the people fiddle for her or have them read her palm, baffling many an old Gypsy woman by turning the tables and telling their fortune, which these crones did not appreciate. Each to his own: this was the only thing that the Gypsies and footmen were agreed upon.

*

Charlotte was probably waiting by the phone. I ought to have called and said that I wanted to be on my own for a few days. She wouldn't have understood – how could she if I didn't tell her the truth? – and soon would have been ringing at my doorbell. The truth. The truth was that I'd visited the sex museum without her. She'd always wanted to go to the sex museum with me; she'd been talking about it for years. I'd have to go again and pretend it was my first visit. Sink once more into contemplation of the brightly coloured penises. Actually, why not? Charlotte isn't thin, she's got a powerful, well-proportioned body with pronounced hips and thighs. I was never bothered by other women not looking thin. On the contrary, I liked them being a little rounder. It was just pregnant women I couldn't stand, with their overladen, gross bodies, which they proudly flaunted to all and sundry. That belly which kept growing bigger, which dominated all else, the triumph of proliferating flesh, spreading obscenely over the bones and covering everything. I, on the other hand, wanted to be pale and starved. Whenever my grandfather said how terrible I looked, like a skeleton or concentration-camp victim, I took it as a compliment, without the slightest understanding of how malicious the expression *concentration-camp victim* was. If my grandmother heard this she'd say, *Oh, come on, Josef.* By that she meant that you couldn't compare me, her granddaughter, to concentration-camp inmates, *those poor devils.* However, the more sunken my cheeks and the darker the rings around my eyes, the more I felt content. If my grandmother said I looked well, so healthy and with such round cheeks, I felt ill and bloated. Her ideal of beauty came from another era. I did not wish to be associated with food. I harboured the permanent desire to fall unconscious, but I never managed a proper blackout, only two or three instances of circulation problems with dizziness. I wanted to melt into thin air, vanish like a fugitive essence that dissipates the moment it comes into contact with food. I kept thinking of the consumptive women in literature, pale and delicate and thin, and forever passing out even if they did nothing all day – as in Thomas Mann's *Magic Mountain* – except eat (the patients were served five meals per day: huge break-fasts, lunches and dinners with several courses and two snacks in between, because otherwise they would lose too much protein – I was particularly fascinated by this symptom of tuberculosis) and lie on sun terraces, 1,600 metres up, wrapped in furs and camel-hair blankets. They were given smelling salts, held in people's arms or laid down on sofas. Then they were taken to their afternoon tea, where they would be offered milk or hot chocolate and large slices of fruitcake with a thick layer of butter. Five or six times I picked up the receiver and replaced it again. Charlotte mustn't find out anything. I could only tell her about Frau Hohenembs. But even that would baffle her. Why had I spent my Saturday afternoon in the Prater with two elderly ladies I didn't know? Because you can't ever say no, Charlotte would answer. She always accused me of never being able to say no, of being sucked into everything, of being used in every way possible, of allowing myself to be saddled with everything to my own disadvantage, just because I couldn't say no, out of politeness or misconstrued friendliness, which in truth was no more than coward-ice. Frau Hohenembs had wanted to organize another get-together, this time in the Lainzer Tiergarten, which I had declined. So I was able to say no. After our visit to the sex museum we'd gone for a couple of beers in a pub. It was Frau Hohenembs's regular haunt whenever she and Ida went to the Prater. The copper whale on the roof, covered with verdigris, reminded her of her past sea voyages. Although she'd never seen a whale, she had often spied dolphins off the Greek islands and the African coast. In her house on Corfu she'd chosen the dolphin as the heraldic animal to put on her crockery, bedclothes and letter-writing paper. Unfortunately, barely any of this was left; things had disappeared over the years, as they tended to – something breaks, something else is stolen. If Ida were to get the house she'd have to kit it out again from scratch. But she didn't need much, dear Ida. She was a great deal more modest than herself, Frau Hohenembs added. You've been promising me Corfu for thirty years, Ida had snorted, briefly sitting up straight before sinking back down again, holding on to her glass. She had ordered a schnapps to accompany each of her beers. In front of the astonished waiter she sank the shot glass in her beer mug, describing the resulting drink as a submarine. In the meantime, Frau Hohenembs suggested one date after another for our next meeting. I cited urgent and unpredictable work as an excuse, which was partly true; I had to visit a new client the following week and didn't know what would come of it. The firm I occasionally worked for, Hoarders Unlimited, had put me in contact with the

man and described him as a serious case. Others refuse
to believe just how many people are incapable of keeping their homes in a habitable state and are grateful for
outside help, even though they feel ashamed at the same
time. Clearing out clutter, getting rid of superfluous
stuff within the shortest possible time, was the only
thing I'd learned how to do. After all, I'd always had to
remove the traces of my eating and puking as quickly
as I could. The man had sounded utterly desperate on
the phone; his flat was overflowing with old catalogues,
magazines and mail-order goods he'd never opened; his
daughter used to help him tidy up and chuck away, but
she'd emigrated to Australia, came back only once a year
and of course didn't have any time for that sort of thing
(*You can't begin to imagine!* Couldn't I?) I paced up and
down my flat. It was Saturday evening and in the fridge
were two squeezed-out tubes of mustard and a bottle of
ketchup. Upstairs the usual crashing, which made the
doors rattle on their hinges. I thought about being sick,
but the picnic was too long ago. A squeamish aversion
to the stench of semi-digested food prevented me from
doing so. I'd been weaned off it for too long. My body
was demanding to be filled up and then emptied again.
I went from room to room, opened cupboard doors,
looked in drawers, folded items of clothing or tossed
them into the washing basket. If I passed the fridge I
checked to see that I hadn't overlooked anything edible.
The childhood cakes, straight from the oven, the potatoes mashed with gravy – these didn't exist any more.

Strawberry jam cooked up for hours with fruit from our own garden, spreading the walnuts out on the kitchen table with both hands, the silent shelling of the large runner beans. Thrusting your hands into a bowl of the colourfully speckled beans and letting them run through your fingers. Picking the little, round currants from the branches, a game of patience that, in combination with the blazing summer sun, could put you into a trance. Being sent into the garden to fetch parsley and (for the hundredth time) coming back with carrot tops. Going to the vegetable patch with a bowl to fetch peppers and salad for lunch. The bolted lettuces, which against my better judgement I insisted on calling lattices. The certainty that today, tomorrow and the day after lunch would be on the table at twelve. I hadn't come down so far in the world, thank God, that I was forced to make myself porridge out of polenta flour or oats. I hit upon the superb idea of getting drunk. That was the way out! Charlotte couldn't raise any objections, either.

*

In her album of beauty she collected photographs of women from all over Europe. My kedvesem did not discriminate on the basis of class; she was just as happy with a Tuscan peasant girl as she was with the countess from St Petersburg. Lola Montez and George Sand were there, both in stages of advanced, mature beauty. But the main focus of the album was her sister

Marie, ex-Queen of Naples; there were more portraits
of her than anyone else. The two looked so similar,
the same melancholy beauty was typical of both. The
ex-queen dressed far more eccentrically than my dove,
disapproving of simple elegance. My kedvesem had
not included any pictures of herself, but with her grace
she outshone all others like the majestic morning star.
Austrian diplomats were instructed to send portraits
from the upper classes in the cities where they were
posted. Photographs of aristocratic women, all in the
same studio setting, came from everywhere. The ambas-
sador in Turkey was an exception to this rule. He sent
pictures of exotic women from uncertain backgrounds,
wearing pantaloons, short embroidered jackets and
velvet slippers, as if they had come straight from the
harem. In an accompanying letter he expressed his regret
that the upper-class Turkish women, save for a few,
refused to be photographed; not even their husbands
could persuade them. I actually think that the Turkish
men had their own objections and forbade their wives
to have their picture taken. From Paris, on the other
hand, came scandalous likenesses of artistes, actresses
and ballet dancers in their professional wear, short skirts
or even tight-fitting trousers that hid nothing. They
appealed to her love of the circus and vaudeville; she
was unperturbed; in fact she took particular delight in
these photographs.

*

Frau Hohenembs waved me over and explained to me the function of the duck presses. They had been imported from France, where they were used for the dish canard au sang. After the meat had been carved from the bone, the remaining carcasses were pressed to extract the juices. These devices resembled the large citrus presses used in coffee houses and bars, although the handles for pressing down the carcasses were bigger and looked more merciless. They reminded me of compact thumbscrews. In the past they used such gadgets to press raw veal and beef, and drink the juices, seasoned with salt and pepper, sometimes raw, sometimes cooked. This helped, she said, if you didn't want to become too strong, by which I'm sure she meant fat. It was nourishing, too, she added, and staved off the feeling of hunger for a good while. But she couldn't drink it any more as sadly she no longer had a single duck press in her possession. These days she had to make do with simple bouillon – something even Ida was capable of rustling up. She had often thought about making off with one of the presses; it didn't seem especially difficult to steal something from a museum. Particularly here, where there was no cloakroom and people were channelled through the exhibition rooms with their bags. And ever since the testimony of the Cellini Salt Cellar thief, she continued, we know that CCTV monitors aren't always being watched. Besides, it was essentially her property. I asked what she meant by that. She said she couldn't explain now, but the duck presses belonged to her. She looked at me. I was carrying a medium-sized bag into which all four duck presses would fit comfortably, as I suddenly realized. The presses stood beneath a glass dome, which presumably would set off an alarm the moment it was lifted. Frau Hohenembs gently stroked the edge of the glass with her fingers and raised it cautiously to begin with. Open your bag, she whispered, taking the dome with both hands and lifting it right up. Now Ida was there; she took over the job of holding the glass cover while Frau Hohenembs grabbed the largest of the duck presses and put it at the bottom of my bag, which, obeying her orders, I'd opened and was holding out to her. She arranged the other presses to make it look as if they'd always stood there in a group of three, and removed one of the labels, which she slipped into her dress. Ida carefully placed the protective glass dome back down. Zip up the bag, Frau Hohenembs hissed, and I did. At that very moment my mobile rang. I had to open my bag again, it kept ringing, on the screen was a number I didn't know – probably Charlotte using a different phone. My hand trembling, I cut off the call. She would realize, of course, that I had deliberately refused to take it. I'd have to lie to her. No getting into a flap now, Frau Hohenembs said, and we proceeded calmly to the exit. She went ahead, with Ida and me following on behind. Taking my arm, Ida supported and more or less guided me out. On the other side of my body I was clutching the bag, which was leaden. I felt as old and decrepit as the two other women. On my own I wouldn't have managed a single step; I would have sat on the floor and waited until they carried me out, to prison, to hospital, to the Fools' Tower, wherever. We made it to the exit unnoticed and onto a staircase with runners of red coconut matting. A young man with a kepi sat on the third step from the bottom, reading a book. It was a paperback and he clamped the pages he'd read so tightly to the back of the book that the spine must have been broken several times. A name tag was attached to the pocket of his left breast: Johannes. As we passed him he looked up briefly from his book and gave us a friendly Goodbye. We hurried down two floors and, noticing the office of the arts minister, it struck me that stealing the duck press was probably easier than securing an appointment with the minister to give it back. We moved speedily away from the Hofburg towards Karlsplatz, where we boarded a tram. Ida helped me with the bag. After two stops spent in silence, Frau Hohenembs said that I should accompany them to her apartment. She stood beside the two-seater bench where Ida and I were sitting, although all the other seats were free. I detected a poorly suppressed cheerfulness in her voice; indeed she was giggling to herself, trying to keep her mouth shut with her hand. Ida peered melancholically out of the window. She was probably thinking of the nauseating process she'd have to carry out to extract the meat juice and the laborious business of cleaning the press, which was necessary to avoid the place being immediately overwhelmed by a rotting stench. The sooner I was rid of this object the better. Once inside her apartment I took the press out of my bag, placed it on a table and made for the hallway without saying goodbye. With his tall body, the Irish wolfhound stood in my way, preventing me from leaving. Won't you try a glass of meat juice? Ida, get some veal cutlets, quickly! Frau Hohenembs called out, adding, You'll be amazed! Clambering awkwardly over the dog, I slammed the door behind me, without checking to see whether his muzzle was in the way. I was close to tears. I took a stroll in the little park opposite my flat. The bag, now light again, too light, swung back and forth, knocked between my legs and tripped me up. It will take its revenge later, this bag's lightness, I thought, seeing myself gluing equally light paper bags in prison. I sat on a bench and gazed up at my windows, four mirrors dazzling in the sunshine, impossible to see whether anyone was behind them, searching the flat or watching me stare up. No one else in the park was looking at my windows. A few homeless people sat at one of the wooden tables, passing round a two-litre bottle of red wine. Mothers stood at the edge of the sandpit, taking care that their children didn't dig with other children's spades. Pigeons were shooed away, which didn't stop them from coming back again undeterred. A normal summer weekday afternoon in a normal, slightly down-at-heel park. The police couldn't be in my flat, impossible, I thought. No one saw us, no one followed; even if we had been observed no one knew who we were, let alone where we lived. Besides, the duck press was in her apartment, and at my place there was not a shred of evidence pointing to the existence of any Frau Hohenembs. Having said that, she and Ida were highly conspicuous figures who could easily be recognized any time, by the cashier, the attendants or other visitors to the museum. There was definitely a third woman, they'd say, a nondescript one, we can't remember exactly what she looks like, she wasn't wearing a long, black dress like the other two, she was in normal gear, jeans and T-shirt probably, like all young people these days, how are we meant to remember a face, etc. I emptied the bag onto my lap. The display on my mobile didn't show any new messages or missed calls. There wasn't much else in the bag. I stuffed everything into my trouser pockets, wandered on a little further and threw the bag, my favourite one and a thirtieth-birthday present from Charlotte, into a dustbin. I tried to banish all thoughts of Charlotte. The look she would give me, knitting her eyebrows, if I had to admit to her that I'd left the bag somewhere. Would it have been better, perhaps, if the thing had been stolen, snatched out of my hand, the strap cut?

*

Her habit of entering strangers' houses and apartments used to rankle with the emperor. It was a quirk she did not develop until later in life. Whenever she needed refreshment on one of her epic walks, she would go into the nearest house and ask for a glass of milk and a sandwich. She was almost always given what she asked for; people mostly failed to recognize the empress and of course she never revealed her identity. Only once was she chased away by a woman who refused to tolerate a stranger entering her house and behaving with such impudence. She preferred making surprise and unannounced visits to the courts of Europe, too, thereby causing extreme embarrassment. On one such occasion she was arrested because a guard did not recognize her and she was not accompanied by any ladies-in-waiting. In her black walking dresses – after Rudolf's death she wore nothing but black – she did not look particularly elegant, and thus could easily be mistaken for any old peculiar woman. She would sit for hours at the guardhouse until the misunderstanding was cleared up, requiring the intervention of the devastated marshal of the court. My kedvesem loved little performances like this.

*

In the days that followed I sat alone in my flat, alternating between eating and vomiting, and I never answered the landline when it rang. I no longer felt safe in my own home. Anybody who wanted could call me here and embroil me in something. A Frau Savka from the property-management company reached me on my mobile. I didn't recognize the number and thought it might have been Charlotte using a borrowed phone.

Frau Savka asked whether I'd come to a decision about my flat and if I wanted to extend the contract, which expired at the end of the month. I'd totally forgotten that the contract was coming to an end and I told her that I definitely did want to extend it. After she'd hung up I thought that was a mistake. In my current circumstances obviously it would have been better to move out. But I'd got used to the flat; it was the first one I'd found and renovated on my own. I was attached to the place. My right eye had improved; when I looked in the mirror I could only see a scattering of pink spots. The lymph glands were still swollen and my jaw hurt. I'd closed the blinds on the windows facing the street so that no one could watch me from the park. Citing a contagious illness, I'd cancelled the man whose daughter had emigrated to Australia, postponing our appointment indefinitely. He'd sounded desperate and anger had welled up inside me; couldn't he clear away his rubbish on his own? But the anger was mostly directed towards myself. In spite of the fact that I'd completed my degree, including semesters abroad, it was my job to get rid of other people's junk, while having to listen to stories about their screwed-up lives. And what's more the whole thing had been my own idea, after endless employment applications and abortive interviews, whose only purpose was to give the HR bosses a job in which they could savour their ridiculous power. I'd put the receiver down beside the phone and the man's tirade of misery had turned into a steady drone, interrupted by self-pitying snivelling. After ten minutes, during which I'd tidied and regrouped the objects on my living-room table, I picked up the receiver again and said I had to go now, to the hospital, the isolation unit. Saying goodbye politely, with suppressed hatred, I hung up. What were these people really thinking? Charlotte was clearly hurt and waiting for me to call. Twice someone had come to my door and knocked. Both times I was kneeling by the toilet bowl. I paused what I was doing and hardly dared breathe. I felt like a criminal. The interruption was like a sucker punch to my half-emptied stomach. I could hear the blood rushing to my ears. Although I'd thrown up silently I didn't move from where I was, afraid that the person outside might detect a creaking or breathing. I dismissed the idea that it could have been Charlotte at the door. After everything I'd done she would never have condescended to that. It took a lot of hard practice to learn how to vomit silently. I began by sticking down my throat toothbrushes, paintbrushes or ostrich plumes, which I'd bought specifically for this purpose having read that these were what the ancient Romans used. I had no success with my fingers as I couldn't poke them down far enough, to the area where the vomiting reflex begins. I was unable, however, to spare myself the grazed and ultimately scarred knuckles that result from constantly rubbing the roof of one's mouth, because I tried it over and over again. The handles chafed my throat until it bled, and that always gave me such a shock that I'd interrupt my puking. Which meant that not everything came out. I'd try again with my fingers, which never worked. The ostrich feathers always got dirty after the first attempt, and what's more they cost the same as three or four food shops and were never easy to get hold of. After once watching our cat crouch on the living-room carpet and retch, throwing up perfectly round balls of grass, accompanied by miserable staccato noises, I tried to copy her and practised gagging. Although my initial attempts made a dreadful racket, by the end I had perfected the art and was no longer audible, which meant I was able at any time, even when my parents were in the neighbouring bathroom, to disgorge the contents of my stomach unassisted. In fact the cat made louder noises with her grass balls than I did. I must not have eaten more than an hour beforehand, however, and I had to drink a lot of liquid, otherwise the retching wouldn't work. Whenever the cat noticed me throwing up, she would creep under the living-room sofa as if she wanted nothing to do with it, as if she were secretly implicated. Once the footsteps had moved away from my front door I relaxed and emptied my stomach completely. The police would have been more aggressive; I expect the officers would have broken down the door had they entertained suspicions against me. Under the pretext of *exigent circumstances* they can do whatever they like. After rinsing out my mouth and washing my face with cold water, I opened the door to see if anything had been left for me. There was neither a private letter nor any official communication, nothing suggesting any action on behalf of the authorities. There were no reports on telly or the radio of a theft in the Hofburg. I couldn't find anything in the online newspapers either. I hadn't dared to search for 'duck press' directly, for fear of leaving a trail. Even clicking on one or a few articles about it would have been risky. And I didn't want to go to an internet café. Was it really possible that nobody had noticed? Who would remember exactly whether three or four of the things were under the glass, especially as there were only three labels? Three or four, I don't know, I never counted them, definitely more than two, that's all I can say for sure. I had to hand it to Frau Hohenembs, removing the fourth label had been a masterstroke. There must be inventories somewhere. But I bet they weren't checked on a daily basis; they probably never were, that's assuming they could be found in the first place. Perhaps a duck press like that wasn't spectacular enough for the newspapers; after all, it was only a hundred-year-old kitchen gadget, not a work of art. But it was a curio. Or had the theft not been made public deliberately, to lure the culprits into a false sense of security? Pedlars, people checking TV licences or Jehovah's Witnesses – I mustn't drive myself mad. How long could I hunker down in the flat? I was gradually running out of food, and from upstairs came an alarming din again. This time it was dark bass tones droning through the walls and rattling the doors, as if a dance café had opened above me. On my way to the loo I noticed a folded white piece of paper that had been slid under my front door. I recalled the anonymous notes or those with fake signatures that were slipped to me under the desk in class at primary school, or which I found in my coat pocket or school bag. Full of shame, my head burning, I would go to the loo to read these secret messages in a locked cubicle, and keep them at home in a scratched plastic Benco bottle with a faded label. This showed a three-part comic strip extolling Benco's power of invigoration, similar to the effect that tinned spinach had on Popeye the Sailor Man. I would regularly dip into the bottle and pull out a note, as if picking a raffle winner. Then I'd attempt to recognize the clumsily disguised handwriting and thereby identify the real writer. Some words I didn't understand, but when I tried to look them up I couldn't find them in any dictionary or encyclopedia. Either that or they told me nothing if I did find them (for example, 'hump') because the one definition needed to decipher the message wasn't given, and I couldn't infer anything from the other meanings. All I suspected was that they described something inaccessible to me, but at that age I found them more exciting than anything else. I'd spend hours with these well-thumbed letters, and afterwards felt fresh and invigorated, as if I'd just drunk a glass of milk with powdered chocolate or eaten a can of spinach. It was a great disappointment if I came home without a cryptic message or a burning head. My first impulse was to push the note back out of my flat. Then I ignored it for two visits to the loo, but finally curiosity won out. If only I'd flushed it away immediately! This piece of paper contained no secret erotic message, which would have been worth decoding, nor did it invigorate me in the slightest. On the contrary, it only left me despondent. *Please call 55 60 600 as soon as possible. Yours, Frau Hohenembs.* I anticipated that this brazenly requested conversation would be about the duck press. Of course, I should have guessed that it was Ida creeping round my door, irresponsibly putting me in danger. I had no intention of calling. But I suspected Frau Hohenembs would not give up; she'd probably make Ida camp outside my flat until we'd spoken. Carefully adjusting one of the venetian blinds, I peered through the horizontal slats at the park over the road, but didn't see anything suspicious. Only that the blinds urgently needed cleaning. A young woman was sitting on a bench with several supermarket shopping bags. She was looking vacantly up at my windows. Either she seemed to be pondering something or she was just staring *into thin air*, as people put it so nicely. I had the unpleasant impression that she looked similar to me, even though she was too far away for me to be able to see her features properly. There was something in the way she sat that unsettled me; it could have been me sitting there like that. Otherwise the usual mothers with their usual children and the usual homeless people with their usual bottle of wine were going about their usual business. Ida was nowhere to be seen.

*

My first glimpse of the new statue in Vienna's Volksgarten was a shock. Now the Viennese had finally got what they had always wanted – to nail down my proud gull to the city and force her to sit there quietly and wait as events unfolded. They retaliated to her journeying by rail and boat with this stone statue, which is the very opposite of her. As if those responsible had been deliberating for years as to how they could best disconcert my poor petal. They could have at least chiselled her a horse to sit on; that would have been an acceptable compromise. What must have annoyed them most of all was that she never had chairs in her vicinity. Sitting around for hours, as the Viennese love to do, in coffee houses, in wine taverns or on window seats, to watch people and the world go by, was not her thing. The three hours a day she was stuck on a chair during the laborious procedure of dressing her hair was enough for one day. Moreover, this sculpture is a pale imitation of the Maria Theresia statue. Although she is seated too, in her matronly posture the old mother of the people nonetheless manages to execute a movement, and her figure as a whole exhibits a keen sense of vitality, whereas my édes lelkem sits there cowed, hands in her lap, with a book by her knees, utterly passive, almost curled up into herself, her hair a crude jumble on her head – poor Fanny Feifalik, that is no crown braid! – her dress preposterous, and with the most boring facial features you could possibly imagine. My sweet, sweet petal, she did not deserve that.

*

Ida was carrying a blue rucksack, which she laid at the base of the Empress Elisabeth statue in the Volksgarten. She'd slipped another three notes under my door, each bearing the same message and telephone number; I tore them all up and flushed them down the loo. Then I'd heard a scratching sound outside, a dragging and pushing, a creaking then a sigh, finally a flapping, like someone idly leafing through a magazine. As I put my ear to the door and listened to the noise, I could also hear rustling. After a while I opened up and there lay Ida on a camp bed, beside her an open bag, out of the top of which poked a Thermos flask and some rolls wrapped in cling film. The smell of schnitzel hung in the air. Her legs were wrapped in a blanket and on her tummy was an opened bar of chocolate. She told me she'd been instructed to wait here until I'd rung Frau Hohenembs. I slammed the door shut. As far as I was concerned she could lie there till kingdom come. But I didn't have any peace; Ida's presence outside my front door made me nervous, and who could tell what the neighbours might think or whether one of them would call the police? In any case, she would cause a stir by being there, a most unseemly state of affairs. I paced up and down my flat in despair. Eventually I felt worn out and rang Frau Hohenembs. She picked up after two rings. The conversation was as brief as it was unpleasant. I could hear the dog whining in the background, or was it the parrots? I was nervous, and when I'm nervous or agitated I'm practically incapable of communicating. If everything's all right I speak in a nice voice like a professional radio presenter; if not I stutter so badly it's as if I can't even speak my own language. At university I was once asked whether I was a foreigner, because I didn't express myself quickly enough or with the appropriate words for the situation. Falteringly, I asked Frau Hohenembs not to call me again; in her mellifluous Frau Professor German, which had a slight Bavarian twang, she replied that she only wanted to invite me for the occasional walk or museum visit. These were minor, very manageable obligations and I shouldn't worry about being entirely owned by her, that was out of the question. If I refused she would inform the relevant authorities. The expression *being entirely owned by her* shocked me, even if it was out of the question. The idea would never have occurred to me; coming from her, it sounded perfectly natural and made me fear the worst. When I countered that I could just as easily call the police too, she said tersely that, unlike me, she knew what to do. She and Ida were highly unlikely to be prosecuted, especially in Austria. She didn't think I was able to say that about myself. Furthermore, she couldn't imagine that I'd prefer a spell in prison to the occasional hour in her company. The idea was so ludicrous it could never happen, touch wood. She said all this in such a calm voice that I slammed down the receiver, ran out of the room and would have fled from the flat – from the whole world, ideally – if the phone hadn't rung again seconds later. I ran back into the room, grabbed the receiver and heard Frau Hohenembs speak again. Touch wood, it shan't be to your disadvantage; I have a most lucrative offer for you. She hung up. Outside my door, a mobile rang. I heard a final rustling, squeaking and dragging and a Goodbye! from Ida. She'd obviously been given the order to strike camp.

Frau Hohenembs walked twice around the stepped site, examined the two stone dogs that lay on either side at the feet of the statue of Empress Elisabeth, and shook her head. The dogs are far too small and the dress – if you can even call it a dress – is impossible, she exclaimed in our direction. Dogs as large as I would like just don't exist. The dress of the Austrian empress, who in her time secured the reputation as an iconic beauty, with painstaking routines for her hair and clothes, was indeed disappointing, a simple loose-fitting garment, held together at the waist by a sort of sash, almost like a tunic, with no decoration or pattern. It could have easily been a linen sheet with sleeves. We stood slightly to one side, Ida picked a few flowers from the border and sang 'White Roses of Corfu' to herself. There were no locals or tourists around, the statue was on the perimeter of the Volksgarten; perhaps it wasn't marked in tourist guides. A narcotic heat shrouded the small area, which seemed removed from time; an indeterminate buzzing pervaded the air, crickets or bees or hummingbirds, and then I heard Frau Hohenembs speak, as if from far away: Give me the fuses, let me do it. The scratching sound of Velcro being opened and then the bang of an explosion. A moment later the statue was a pile of rubble and dust. Standing beside me, Ida took my arm, we dashed out onto the Ringstrasse and just managed to catch a passing tram. A passenger who'd watched us running for the stop was kind enough to press the door button from the inside.

*

If Lucheni had known how great her desire was for death, perhaps he would not have chosen her as his victim. Moreover, she did not match his image of the royal enemy, but he could not have known that either. It had always been her conviction that we had over-reached ourselves, that we no longer fitted in with the world, that it was just a question of time until humanity finally sent us packing with nothing but rags. Those rags she would have wrapped around her hips in the evening, soaked in cold vinegar because this was purported to tauten the thighs. To begin with she failed to notice that she was mortally wounded. She thought the man had simply knocked her over because she was in his way, even though he had in fact rushed at both of them, Countess Sztáray and her. She even went onto the boat. It was only on board that she sensed something was wrong, terribly wrong.

*

Three days had passed since the attack on the statue and there was still no sign of Ida. Even though I didn't miss her, it made me nervous. Being in contact with Ida meant unpleasantness; not being in contact meant uncertainty and waiting. This time the internet was full of reports; sitting hunched and apprehensively at my computer, I scrolled through the news as if this approach might disguise my traces on the Web. *Madman Blows up Empress Sissi Statue, Another Cowardly Attack on our Sissi, Booby Trap in Volksgarten* – these were the headlines. I reassured myself with the thought that my interest in these articles would not be particularly suspicious; they were the lead stories for the news sites and most Viennese probably read them. There was all manner of conjecture about the incident. Evidently no one had seen us, although we'd behaved so conspicuously. In their old-fashioned black clothes they must have looked even more conspicuous next to me, who'd been dressed *normally*. A lone male culprit, possibly a critic of the defunct Monarchy and a misogynist, sexually frustrated, this was the view of most of the daily papers. Or the opposite, a supporter of the Monarchy, who regarded Sissi as an anarchistic element who accelerated the downfall of Imperial Austria. Very few drew parallels with Luigi Lucheni, the man who stabbed the real Sissi with a sharpened needle file in Geneva. In the absence of the Prince of Orléans, whom he'd actually

wanted to kill (the prince himself being a substitute for
Lucheni's favoured target, King Umberto of Italy, ruled
out because Lucheni didn't have the money for a ticket
to Italy) he made do with Sissi, because she happened to
be near to him that day, plus she was an empress. I also
read online that the dynamite attack had probably been
a sort of ersatz murder, a mix-up, an accident or – and
this seemed plausible too – the rehearsal for an attack
on a living person. It would never occur to Charlotte
that I might be involved. We'd joke about it later; over
a glass of wine I'd tell her how I'd unwillingly become
an accomplice in this crime. But now I whiled away the
time getting rid of food, although *whiling away* is in
fact the wrong term here. Ever since I'd started again,
time was passing so quickly, as if someone was in the
room next door, devouring the hours from me. In truth
this someone was myself; I was eating away my hours,
gobbling them down at lightning speed. In next to no
time I polished off the last of my savings. My father
always used to say that I might as well chuck straight
down the loo the money I spent on food – or the food
itself, without taking the detour of my body. It would
be healthier for my organism and show me how absurd
my behaviour was. I ought to have followed his advice.
The paralysing emptiness that sometimes grips the ex-
junkie, and the feeling that when the addiction dies part
of the I dies along with it, were nowhere to be seen; I was
more animated than I had been in ages and constantly
had something to do. I'd only been outside once, with

my checked shopping trolley, to buy newspapers and unhealthy foodstuffs. I indulged in so many products that hadn't existed twenty years ago, particularly not in XXL family sizes. When I ate, I was my own family. Finally I could give in to the temptation that so many different foods had exerted on me for years, but which had always been taboo because they were too industrial (microwave ready-meals), too fatty (filo pastry with cheese, chocolate sauce, crisps), too sweet and too soft (plaited buns, oversized cream puffs, apple strudel). I loaded up the trolley with gastronomic delights. I didn't care what the cost was, so long as the cashpoint still spat out money. It had to be this way. Never in my life had I done such a monstrous shop. I wondered whether people could tell the real reason behind what I was buying. I looked at the other shoppers defiantly and primed myself for defence. They were all so preoccupied with what they were doing that they wouldn't have noticed if I'd piled my trolley high with slabs of bloody meat. I then had an unpleasant experience at the checkout. A supermarket detective in a beige trench coat asked me to open my handbag. He reminded me of the anonymous figure from the advertising campaign for a large supermarket chain, although that character had only ever appeared as a black shadow. Not aware of having done anything wrong, I thought this was just a random check and so opened my bag unsuspectingly. Inside were three shiny tins of caviar, each 250 grams. Erm, um, erm, I began to stutter, I-I've no i-idea how they got into my bag, I never eat caviar, I can't stand the stuff (I hate it when the tiny balls burst in your mouth and I also hate the intrusive fishy, salty taste). Someone must have planted them on me. I pointed to the contents of my trolley; I'd bought so much that I'd hardly run a risk like that just for three tins (even if they were the most expensive things in the shop). The woman waiting behind me came to my assistance; she'd seen a squat old lady wearing a peasant-style headscarf fiddle with my handbag while I was spending ages in the baked-goods section. I looked at her in astonishment. Why didn't you say anything, then? I asked. She turned red and shrugged. I didn't want to get involved, she murmured. The old woman looked so down-at-heel, I thought she wanted to steal a bit of cash for something to eat. I was speechless. In the end I was saved by the cashier: This woman's been coming here for years. Why would she start stealing now? I removed the tins from my bag and handed them to the detective. He gave them a thorough examination, twiddling them between his fingers and behaving as if he were reading the Cyrillic writing. Do you really not like caviar? he asked. You might have been going to give it to someone as a gift. I shook my head. And why would someone sneak caviar into your handbag? Was someone trying to play a trick on you? I shrugged my shoulders. I was exhausted. I just wanted to be alone with my food. Eventually he let me go; maybe he didn't fancy notifying the police. Not wanting to hang around, I left the shop. It was the last time I'd be going to that supermarket.

*

She was amazed that people cheered her when she appeared in public. That they gawked and called out to her when she did her neck-breaking riding exercises. Grateful for a fleeting glance. She was always accused of caring about nothing, of showing no interest in government business. They took exception to her engagement with my homeland, after which her energy was exhausted. What else should she have done? Her son knew that the Monarchy's time was up. And that it would not end without bloodshed. His farewell letters to his sister and her were quite clear. It just took a little longer than he had thought. And his daughter took a socialist as her second husband! No one would have imagined that this pale Belgian child could have caused such a scandal in the family. Szeretett angyalom, how difficult your life had already been made when your brother married the actress. And then that. Your granddaughter!

*

I was learning a new vomiting technique and was eating by colours. I started with chemical sweets such as bright-green gummy frogs or pink foam bacon bits or claret so-called laces and snakes. These took time to mix with the mush of food that followed, which meant that my vomiting could be monitored. I would puke until I'd arrived at this tough, lurid mass, so I could be sure I'd got everything out. I always ate chocolate, ice cream, or cakes and tarts at the end, so that these things would be regurgitated first of all. This gave me the guarantee that they'd be completely out of my body. It was the ideal scenario, which is only possible, of course, if you've got the time. In my *break times*, that's to say those short periods when I wasn't eating or vomiting, I trawled the internet for news about the explosion. The analysis of the surviving shreds from Ida's rucksack had revealed nothing, except for the fact that it was an Eastpak rucksack, which was probably used by a hundred thousand people in Vienna alone. Or I lay on the sofa and let the television anaesthetize me, or browsed the papers and drank litres of jasmine tea to stop myself from becoming totally dehydrated. I fancied I was giving my body a detox. I calculated my body mass index and took my measurements. Only on the hips had I reached the stipulated benchmark of ninety centimetres. My waist was still too big, way off sixty, over seventy! My chest was a few centimetres over ninety; for my liking it could have been smaller, but that wasn't so important. Only the waist counted. I'd put the scales beside the fridge; once again they were my only point of reference in the world. I'd already lost two kilos! I felt fresher and lighter than I had in ages. My waist would get smaller in good time! It was a shame that lacing up was no longer practised. If I could be sewn into clothes I'd soon have the ideal waist. That would be more effective than wearing things that were too tight, like Karl Lagerfeld, who kept his weight down this way. During the course of those three days I stood on the scales more times than I had done in all the years before. Often I'd leap up in the middle of reading the newspaper or watching an advertisement for diet products, stand on the scales and prove to myself that I hadn't shifted a gram either way since the previous weigh-in fifteen minutes earlier. This was mostly true, but sometimes I'd suddenly be half a kilo or even a whole kilo more, which made me check my weight three further times, one after another. I attributed the increase to the enormous volume of tea I was pouring down myself, even though I had to pee just as often. Something wasn't working. I stood in front of the mirror to check my bare tummy. I cried. It was too big. It's always too big and if you're thin it's never flat, it always curves outwards, bloated, forming rolls when you sit. Hanging over the band of your knickers. Swelling to twice its size unless you've fasted the whole day, then the upper half of the tummy is acceptable, but the lower part is still too big. A glance in the mirror: the tummy's still there. Even if I tell myself, My tummy's quite normal, no washboard, but a tummy that has to accommodate metres and metres of intestines, I still have a fundamental hatred of it. It's always to blame, two, three kilos more, obviously on the tummy. It's the home of gluttony, always hungry, always wanting something. Forever having to be pulled in. It makes the brain a slave, forcing it to think continually of food, cooking, shopping, everything as fatty as possible. It wants butter,

butter, butter. Cream. Fluffy, sweet, yeasty dough. Fatty cheese, rich sauces. A bottomless barrel. I was too nervous to keep calm; only when I was scoffing everything was I able to stay sitting down. I took advantage of my restlessness to tidy up. I'd been sitting in the kitchen and living room; the bedroom alone was free of empty packets and bottles. I hadn't put a foot in there during these three days; I'd slept on the sofa. I slept with the television on, having fetched it up from the cellar. My telly addiction had flared up again. If you watched telly while gorging you could convince yourself that you were doing something more important than eating. On the other hand, television is so dreadful that it's only bearable when accompanied by food. The comfort I'd taken in the past from being connected to the world by television, and being part of it too, was absent these days. There were too many channels; the whole thing was too random. There'd been two or three reports about the explosion, you could see the ruins of the statue, only the plinth had remained intact. An old woman spoke angrily into a large microphone: Wasn't it enough that poor Sissi had been so gruesomely murdered? She'd never done anyone any harm, this noble lady, and she'd suffered enough already, so why someone had to go and desecrate her statue now, she was ashamed of being Austrian, that sort of thing wouldn't have happened in Germany, there they know how to treat people like Sissi. It was probably the Italians again, she went on, what can you do about it, the EU lets anyone go where they like, even though it's common knowledge how much the Italians hated us. At the time of the Monarchy they even called for a smoking boycott to damage the Austrian tobacco monopoly, that says it all, doesn't it, if the Italians decide to give up smoking. The microphone was prised from her hands, then a clip was played and a man dressed as Punch announced the weather forecast. Punch's job was clearly to confuse the viewers so that by the end your head would be swimming with downpours and instances of the sun breaking through as well as highs and lows and you'd have no idea what the weather was actually going to be like and what to put on if you decided, or were forced, to leave your flat. I, at any rate, had no plans to step outdoors.

*

In the 1980s the Swiss government sent the head of Luigi Lucheni, preserved in formaldehyde, to the Museum of Pathology and Anatomy in Vienna, the 'Fools' Tower', on the condition that it would not be exhibited, to avoid feeding the population's appetite for sensationalism. The Swiss wanted to rid themselves of all memories of the assassin. Nobody knows why they declined to bury the head with the rest of the body; indeed, it remains a mystery why they cut it off in the first place. Perhaps they wanted to squeeze something out of the head, an untold secret explaining everything that was absent from the writings left behind. But as the Viennese had no idea what to do with the head – there was nothing more to be got from it and they were not permitted to exhibit it – some years ago they wanted to burn the thing and bury the ashes in Vienna Central Cemetery. She spoke of the head all the time. She was obsessed by it. When Lucheni pounced on her she could barely see him and he vanished a moment later. Sometimes I think she ran into the murder weapon on purpose; she did nothing to protect herself. Who can say? Certainly not poor Countess Sztáray, who tried to jump in the way. She often said how she would like to stand facing his head in a glass jar. My proud, cold-blooded kedvesem, per-haps she can get in contact with him.

*

We'll pick you up at ten tomorrow morning. We're going to the Fools' Tower. Ida hung up, I wasn't able to say yes or no any longer. I dragged myself back into the bathroom to continue puking until I felt totally empty. It was seven in the evening; I'd spent the entire day between the sofa and the toilet bowl, and had been stuck in this loop for a week now, uninterrupted by any other activity apart from two shopping trips. Quivering and with my heart pounding wildly, I lay down on the sofa and stared at the telly without taking in what was happening. I'd strained so hard the last time that tears were running down my cheeks. I didn't even get on the scales again. I groaned out loud. My stomach felt as if there were a vacuum inside it. I imagined it like a compressed plastic bag. The thought of our *appointment* pleased me and I didn't care what was going to happen tomorrow, whether we razed the old asylum or plundered it. The important thing was to get out of the flat, which I'd turned into a rubbish dump. Then it occurred to me that the Museum of Pathology's collection in the tower was only open to the public two days a week and would be closed tomorrow. I knew that from Charlotte, who'd worked there years ago as an attendant. Blowing up such a large and solid building would surely need more dynamite than could be carried in a rucksack. And what about the people inside? There were employees looking after the preserved specimens and medical students drawing them. Charlotte used to wear a white coat, like Ida when she waited on Frau Hohenembs. She would have fun scaring friends who came to visit her in the museum. She'd hide behind a door and jump out, or jangle her bunch of keys beside the huge, slightly stained, marble mortuary slab and smile as she pointed out the drain hole in the middle, through which the bodily fluids of the corpses flowed. If you looked away in disgust, you'd see a second mortuary slab in the cell next door, on which the contours of a body could be discerned beneath a white sheet. Yellowish hair stuck out at one end, yellowish feet at the other, and behind was a wall full of drawers needing no further explanation. The round building with its rooms arranged in a circular layout (these were once cells in which the mentally ill were chained up) was home to glass jars of deformed children's heads and children's bodies, crooked skeletons, old medical instruments – including a dental practice from the late nineteenth to early twentieth century – and wax moulages, lifelike replicas of diseased or deformed organs and body parts. I wanted to get up from the sofa to make myself a camomile tea, but my knees gave out. For a while I stayed where I was, motionless. Then at some point I toppled over and fell into a deep sleep, which was more like a blackout. I didn't wake up till the following morning; it was six o'clock and my limbs ached as if they'd been battered. I could barely see out of my eyes, my stomach ached, my head hurt and I had a terrible thirst. Eventually I made a camomile tea and stood on the scales – four kilos lighter than the previous week. In the middle of the chaos I stood there with my cup of tea, surveying the scene. Charlotte would not have been pleased; she was so neat and tidy. And I imagine Hoarders Unlimited would have cancelled my contract there and then. The floor was littered with empty packets. Encrusted plates and cups covered every surface. Below the table lay books about dog breeds and dog magazines. And the smell of sick floating above it all. Oh, Charlotte. It spoke more clearly than anything I could say. I took a shower, letting the water get as hot as I could tolerate, and I promised myself that this had been my last ever relapse. You've got to stop, I insisted, before correcting myself, saying into the spray of water that I had already stopped, That's the very last time! A reminder of the past, so not even a relapse, but a painful commemoration to prevent me from ever falling back into addiction. I spoke to myself as I might do to a sick horse, repeating it again and again and again and again: the mendacious and self-deceitful mantra that I'd deliberately planned the eating binges to be absolutely sure that I wasn't addicted. Forgotten was the hustled compulsion I'd surrendered to, forgotten the automatic eating I didn't think about as I did it. Forgotten, that I'd made use of the most random, banal opportunity to break my abstinence. I'd been offered a Gugelhupf and I'd had nothing better to do than to stuff myself with it. As if I'd merely been waiting for this encounter, like a sleeper who leads a perfectly normal life for decades before being activated by their terrorist cell and blowing up a carriage on the underground. I'd visit the Fools' Tower. Then I'd ask Frau Hohenembs to let me go. Calmly and in plain words, no angry face or insulting accusations, no incriminations, preferably with mock gratitude. I'd lie to her about just how exciting the time I'd spent with her had been and what an interesting person she was. I was convinced that she'd let me go and I felt strong enough to have the conversation. She'd be touched, moved by the childish trust I placed in her, by the fact that I didn't bear any grudge and because I considered her capable of making such a grand gesture to someone who was at her mercy. That must flatter her vanity. In my euphoric state I was desperate to call

Charlotte. But she must never find out about any of this. I was still in my underwear when the bell rang; it was nine o'clock. I put on a dressing gown and opened the door a crack. Putting her whole weight against it, Ida forced her way in, behind her came Frau Hohenembs. With her gloved hands she removed my dressing gown. You've lost weight! Bravo! I blushed. She'd noticed! Then my face turned hot, from anger. Anger at myself. Such comments ought not to affect me any more. You could do with a cleaning lady, she said. She'd made her way into the living room and was taking a look around. Have you had guests? Yes, I replied, as you can see. I haven't got round to clearing up yet. She went up and down the room, inspecting everything thoroughly like an estate agent valuing a flat. She picked up items of clothing and magazines to check whether there was anything lurking underneath, and kicked an empty box beneath the sofa. Show me the other rooms. Ida seemed to be searching for something too; she rummaged among the chocolate wrappers on the table and indeed found a bar with strawberry and cream filling that I had missed. Without asking, she took a bite and continued to delve into the paper and foil. Do you have any milk? Frau Hohenembs called from the kitchen, and while I put on my jeans in the bathroom I could hear the squishing sound of the fridge door being opened. It was closed again. I never had milk.

*

She placed enormous trust in me by giving me the job of setting up a dairy in the Tyrolean Garden of Schönbrunn Park. The milk in Vienna did not meet her demands. A range of different breeds of cow from all over Europe were brought here, as well as goats and chickens. My rose was permanently on the hunt for the perfect milk that would best enhance her beauty and health. Inferior-quality milk could spoil her whole day. From her travels she would often bring back animals whose milk she particularly liked. If she ever went away without me, I had to describe to her at length all the new arrivals of cows that had taken place during her absence. She was interested in the minutest details. Her letters to the emperor were regularly accompanied by instructions for looking after the cows, which he then passed on to me. All the cows that lived and laboured here were scrupulously clean, vaccinated and brimming with milk. Every morning fresh milk, butter, thick cream and coffee cream were delivered to the palace kitchens from the court dairy. They produced soured milk and yoghurt. The emperor and Katharina Schratt, his lady friend, would taste the milk of new animals or new dairy products and had to report back to her. She herself came regularly to the dairy to have a cup of milk; she would sit alone in the rustic Hungarian-style parlour, on rustic red furniture. I'd had the colourful, flowery porcelain brought from Hungary, and was instructed by the milker about every process. The walls were decorated with photographs of Hungarian cows and drawings of various breeds of cattle.

*If she received guests here, the court confectioner had
to serve in traditional Hungarian costume. That milk,
that butter – you cannot find products of such quality
these days. The members of the imperial family and
even His Majesty's lady friend, who received her daily
delivery too, could not get enough of them.*

*

In the grounds of the old hospital where the former
asylum was, nothing had changed. I hadn't been here
in ages. The tall, overgrown meadow had not been
manicured into a smooth lawn. In the days of the
Monarchy the tower had served as a place of confinement for the mentally ill. There was no therapy, but
sometimes cold water was tipped over the inmates or
they were put on a diet, which meant they were left to
starve to keep them calm. I found that very hard to
imagine. You have to be severely weakened by hunger
to be *calm*. Hunger tends to make you nervous. Non-
sterile ropes made of horsehair or women's hair were
rubbed around the back of *patients'* necks until the skin
ulcerated and they developed a fever, which apparently
produced a certain therapeutic effect. Although Charlotte
had not been able to say what. The most troublesome
cases, that's to say the ones who were the most time-
consuming and needed the greatest care, were chained
up all their lives; for this the asylum even had its own
smithy. Later the building was used as a store and

workshop, as accommodation for doctors and nurses, and at some point in the 1970s it was turned into the Museum of Pathology and Anatomy, with its infamous exhibits. The smithy was also preserved as a display room. It's said that the head of the anarchist Lucheni – Sissi's murderer – was housed here for a while, before they decided, probably with reluctance, to bury it. The Fools' Tower reminded me less of a Gugelhupf, as the Viennese used to describe it, and more of an oversized springform tin in which a cake had already risen. The roof was slightly curved and the chimneys around the ring on the inside looked like a raised pastry crust. I was sad that the tower was going to be destroyed. We'll go straight in, Frau Hohenembs said. Ida bought tickets for the first floor, which you could only visit on a guided tour; afterwards we could look at the collection on the ground floor by ourselves. As the Fools' Tower was unexpectedly open, clearly the plan was to make away with an exhibit, I was sure of that. Ida's rucksack looked pretty full, which could be a cover; perhaps she'd put a box inside as protection for the stolen goods and so they wouldn't show through the material. We joined a small group in the courtyard that was waiting for the museum guide. There were no security checks; Ida could go in unimpeded with her rucksack. The guide wore an unbuttoned white doctor's coat, its tails wafting around behind him. He introduced himself as a medical student in the final stage of his studies. He was tall and fair, with a pointed beard projecting from his chin. You could tell that he must have given this talk hundreds of times already. He did not vary his intonation between facts and anecdotes; he reeled everything off in the same, faintly melancholic tone. I'd heard most of it already from Charlotte, who knew the history of all the spectacular preserved specimens. If this student had ever taken pleasure in his work, it was long in the past. I also knew from Charlotte that things had been stolen from here, all sorts of things: kidney stones, wet specimens, bones and bone fragments of all sizes, preserved appendices (taken by young doctors who, even if they weren't surgeons, would proudly present their *first* one to friends). Even a foetus moulded in plastic had been pinched. Animal skulls, of course, the favourites being monkey skulls, which were turned into ashtrays. Charlotte had been interested in a swordfish skull, including the saw, obviously. There were hundreds of these, but she'd never found the opportunity to purloin one. I wondered what Frau Hohenembs was after. Perhaps a rickety child's skeleton or a particularly ghastly moulage with a syphilis deformity, or the cast of a male head with bulbous tumours clustering around the skull like an eccentric bonnet. The facial expression at the moment the cast was taken was serious; a hint of bitterness at the corners of the mouth, the lips narrow and tightly shut, the eyelids lowered, almost submissive. The man seemed resigned to his fate, not at all in despair, although his fellow human beings must have made his life hell. It was the way they were mounted that made the head and face moulages appear especially gloomy. They were hung on the walls like shot and stuffed animals, or antlers. Where part of the back of the head was missing, the model was fixed to a board wrapped in material, making it look as if it was wearing a ruff. This pseudo-collar suggested a disproportionate care, a fake kindness that had been shown to the head or, more accurately, its cast. The face itself was slightly bowed towards the floor, strengthening the impression of humility, or perhaps evoking it in the first place. I suspected that there was something heavy in Ida's rucksack. She was carrying it as if it had some weight. Perhaps the plan was to swap an item, so that the theft would not be immediately apparent. On the first floor, in the collection of moulages and wet specimens, a theft would have been fairly difficult. Our group was watched by two female doctors. When we were in one room, they made sure that everyone went in and everyone came out again; no one was allowed to linger on their own for more than a minute. If we were in a section of the ring-shaped corridor while the student was discussing an exhibit, the two of them opened a cell door at the front and back so that the group remained huddled together like a herd of sheep. This forced us to stand in close proximity; each of us had bodily contact with our neighbours to the front, back and sides. Nothing is worse than the bodies of strangers pressing continually against your own, and it's even worse if these bodies deliberately barge into you, not yielding a single centimetre, but in their quest for space spreading further and further like an insidious cancer. I wiped sweat from my brow with the back of my hand. Whenever the group moved, we were bumped forward. I let myself fall back, which meant I had only a doctor and the cell door behind me, and I heard no more of the guided tour. Frau Hohenembs and Ida fell back too. They were not listening to what the student was saying, but whispering to each other. When the tour finished we could finally go down to the ground floor. The group slowly dispersed. I asked Frau Hohenembs which object we were going to take. She looked at me in surprise. What makes you think that's what we're doing? On the contrary, we're going to leave them a nice present. I just don't know which is the right room for it. Are you planning on blowing up the tower? I asked. What strange ideas you have! Be quiet. You'll find out in good time. I wasn't mistaken: there *was* a heavy object in Ida's rucksack. We had to wander around the exhibition several times before Frau Hohenembs finally decided on a room. The cells on the ground floor were devoted to pictures of diseases and health-related topics. The smithy was in one of the rooms, the old dentist's practice was here too, as well as two *alchemist's chambers*, filled with all sorts of items without which an alchemist is no alchemist: skulls, stuffed animals (from birds to crocodiles), teeth, snakes, skins, feathers, candles, cats, rugs, chests, jars, bottles, receptacles containing all manner of mysterious things. This mishmash curiously stood out from the rest of the exhibition; it looked like medieval magic. Not

like the scientific documentation of disease and devia-
tion from the norm which, according to the brochures
lying around, the museum was dedicated to. This exhibition denounced the Middle Ages as a sinister and
shady period. Frau Hohenembs had chosen the two
rooms because she thought that among so many ominous
exhibits a new one would not be so obvious; it could
simply be left in a dark corner. The only potentially
tricky moment was Ida placing the object swiftly in the
right place without being seen. Frau Hohenembs told
her where it was to go. Ida put the rucksack on the floor
and carefully took out a cylinder-shaped glass container,
having first made sure that there were no visitors nearby.
In the glass container a human head was swimming in
liquid. I clapped a hand over my mouth to stop myself
screaming out loud. Frau Hohenembs instructed me to
stand beside her so that Ida, who'd already slipped under
the rope, would be screened by the two of us. Ida put
the container between a skull and a stuffed owl, and
draped a few feathers around the ensemble. The head
was slightly behind the owl; you could easily miss it at
first glance. I stared spellbound at the specimen. It was
a male head; the liquid it swam in was cloudy, like green
pond water, making the head appear deformed, widen-
ing it. The eyes were half open, the mouth twisted, you
could see his teeth, which seemed to be in good condition. Capital! Frau Hohenembs was utterly delighted.
She looked at the new exhibit. That's exactly how I
imagined it. Bravo, Ida! You're the best. My one and

only! Don't forget Corfu! Ida said. Frau Hohenembs
nodded with her eyes closed. Who *is* it? I asked, and
Frau Hohenembs whispered that it was the head of Luigi
Lucheni, Sissi's murderer, now back in its rightful place.
The head had been here once before, but not made
accessible to the public; the museum hadn't dared exhibit
it. The idea had been to bury the head in the anatomical
graves at the Central Cemetery, but fortunately this plan
had been thwarted. I argued that the display was mis-
leading if nobody knew it was Lucheni. We have to take
that chance; if Ida were to put a label by the head then
there's little chance that the museum would let it stay
here. No, they'd try to bury it again. Like this, it won't
stick out at all. We've seen what it's like in museums;
the staff don't know every exhibit by heart. Maybe they'll
be delighted to discover they've been gifted a new specimen. What's more, the management has changed since
then; the new lot haven't ever seen the Lucheni head, so
they won't recognize it. And as a preserved head is nothing unusual here, they'll accept it without comment, to
avoid any embarrassment. Lucheni fitted perfectly
between the owl and skull; the new director was bound
to think so too. I had my doubts. Even if the museum
management had never seen the head in real life, there
must be images of such a notorious specimen and a file
that every museum director would consult upon taking
up the post. After we'd left the museum I asked Frau
Hohenembs how she'd got hold of the glass container.
As usual when a question didn't suit her, she gave no

reply. According to Ida, the head had been hanging around in her flat for five years, to her persistent horror – she'd had to dust the container every week. The dog would stand in front of it and bark daily, always at the same time in the late morning, and for several minutes. Then he would turn around and leave the room, avoiding it for the rest of the day and not returning till the following morning, to perform the same ritual. Ida herself was fed up of looking at that face; she didn't need to see it any more.

*

Once, for her name day, she asked the emperor for a Bengal tiger, a locket or a lunatic asylum. This last wish satisfied her desire to do something for the befuddled souls who in Vienna were housed in the so-called 'Fools' Tower' in wretched conditions. Chained, left to vegetate on nothing but straw, no better than wild animals, and subjected to obscure, albeit not life-endangering, treatments. Of course, it was terribly prosaic of him to send her a locket by return; he did not even make reference to the other two requests. She used to visit orphanages and hospitals, never held back from touching cholera victims, even when going back to her grandchildren afterwards. She would always arrive unannounced and ask to sample food from the kitchen – my dear rose, who was always so careful about what she ate – thereby making the director despair. Most of all she liked the

*lunatic asylums; once in one of these institutions she
met a woman who thought she was Her Majesty. Mein
kedvesem was shocked, but kept her composure and
later said to me, 'That poor woman, if only she knew!
That I live in a prison just like her.'*

*

All I wanted was camomile tea. I sat on the sofa in the
midst of my rubbish tip, a cup in hand. Something
repeated on me; a vile taste flooded my mouth. Something
was fermenting in my stomach. In the past this had only
happened when I had eaten very heavy things in exces-
sive quantities and was unable to vomit, or would not
allow myself to as a punishment; because yet again I
wanted to stop for good, I would not allow myself to
puke a final time. I thought that was the only way I could
succeed, by breaking the cycle and putting up with this
digestive hell without resorting to the *panacea*. My
stomach would stop digesting. Used to being emptied
artificially on a regular basis, it couldn't deal with these
quantities any more. So the contents would ferment for
days, not going down by a millimetre. As if a stinking
lump had been deposited there. I'd have to burp continually, a foul eggy gas would pour out of my mouth
and I couldn't be among people any more. I would drink
peppermint tea, or very seldom a schnapps, which sometimes helped. When the alcohol smell of the schnapps
mixed with the stench of sulphur, I would belch in a

devastating way. I felt like an ancient, sticky dustbin in which the rubbish was rotting away. If this condition lasted for longer than a couple of days, I would puke again after all, for fear of being poisoned by the sulphurous fumes, but also out of disgust: I couldn't put up with such putrefaction in my body any more. After we'd left the Fools' Tower, Frau Hohenembs had said to me, You did well back there, my dear. I'm very satisfied with you. Unlike Ida, who took advantage of her good mood, and rather than appealing to her generosity and asking her to *let me go*, I walked silently behind the two figures in black. Well, we were going the same way, which was particularly humiliating. It didn't even occur to me to take a different route. When we got off the tram, Frau Hohenembs with her gloved hand and Ida with her empty rucksack both gave me a friendly wave goodbye. I'd never seen the two of them in such good spirits. I started heading towards my flat without really wanting to return home. I didn't know where else to go. I couldn't turn up at Charlotte's. I contemplated what I ought to do and reluctantly came to a clear conclusion, one that had in truth been haunting my mind for a long time, but I'd been suppressing: I really had to talk to Frau Hohenembs. Exactly what I was most terrified of. Ringing and requesting to meet her, just the two of us. In front of Ida I'd find it too embarrassing to have to beg Frau Hohenembs, which is what it ultimately boiled down to. Ida probably didn't care, but her presence would inhibit me. The phone call seemed the most difficult thing, which is why I postponed it till the following day instead of acting right away and exploiting the goodwill of the moment. I thought that if I slept on it and recovered from this day I'd be able to approach the project with fresh vigour and convincing arguments. I failed to consider that this strategy gave Frau Hohenembs time to think up new tasks for me. As soon as I was freed from the clutches of this woman I'd be able to resume my normal life. I could call Charlotte, could work, forget my relapse or see it as a warning that I must never regard myself as safe. I switched on the radio, turned up the volume to maximum, making the speakers buzz, and danced through the flat to the song 'Caught by the Fuzz' by Supergrass, cup of camomile tea still in hand. I twisted and swayed until I was giddy; I was free! Suddenly I was struck by a bitter feeling of hunger. No surprise there. I hadn't kept down the last thing I'd eaten. I rushed to the fridge, then warned myself to be restrained. I held on tight to the handle. Slowly, think about it first! The fridge was empty. I broke into a sweat. I had to watch out. What I ate now was extremely important. It had to be healthy and a normal portion that didn't overburden my body, so better for it to be a smaller than normal portion. I was already so sick with hunger that going shopping seemed an impossibility. Around the corner was an Asian restaurant with an all-you-can-eat offer. Wasn't that bold, in my condition? Shouldn't the first meal in my normal life be something simpler? But equally, I could eat as little as I wanted to in this place. That seemed a good approach. Tiny morsels of each healthy dish or, even better, of two or three dishes, otherwise I'd lose track and get the fatal impression I was pigging out. In any case, I'd always felt inhibited in all-you-can-eat restaurants, so I was unlikely to go off the rails. A large part of the pleasure in eating comes from doing it in private; you don't want anyone watching you. Apart from the quantity you can't eat in the way you'd like to – everything on the table at the same time to avoid any interruptions while you scoff. You really want to immerse yourself in the process of gorging and not have to stand up; you want to be greedy and loud. Which is impossible in a restaurant where there are staff keeping an eye on how much you pile onto your plate, perhaps winking at you or pointing at a dish that you absolutely have to try. It's precisely this invitation to eat – how do you know the waiter isn't stuffing a napkin in his mouth to stop himself from bursting out laughing? – that is deeply shameful. In spite of this you take the risk of eating too much by accident. That could happen very quickly. And then having the willpower to stop at once, refusing to take another mouthful and resisting the feeling of having overeaten, not everyone's capable of that, not even carefree eaters. The manager of Suzie Chang's greeted me at the door and she pointed to the buffet. I nodded and went straight over without finding a table first. I didn't deliberate for very long, taking the last three pieces of salmon sushi along with the parsley garnish – harmless and low in calories. With my plate in hand, only now did I peer around the restaurant; it was half empty and several tables by the window were unoccupied. I ordered a jasmine tea. Then I got a bowl of white rice with broccoli, taking plenty of time over it. After that, a bowl of fried noodles and two slightly chewy dumplings filled with mincemeat. I ate with chopsticks to drag the process out. Although they were chewy, the dim sum tasted excellent so I took three more. Then I was full and started to panic; I had planned to stop eating before I was full, hadn't I? I turned over in my mind what I'd eaten. It wasn't that much in fact, it only seemed like it: I just wasn't used to keeping anything in my stomach. The sushi, rice and broccoli were innocuous, and the fried noodles and dumplings (fried too), oh well. A little fat, perhaps, and three dumplings rather than five would have sufficed, but it was still within the realms of normal. In any case, I was absolutely starving. I gestured to the manager for the bill. I drank my plum wine and went home with a full tummy, but not unhappy. Standing by my door were a woman and two men, one of whom was ringing the bell. My first instinct was to run away. They've got me now, I thought; who could they be other than the police? But it was too late to run away; the woman had already noticed me and was smiling. What do you want? I asked, my mouth dry and the snap of the handcuffs already echoing in my ears. The man who rang the bell turned around. Hello, I'm from Hustler Property Management. I've got a viewing in Flat 4. Are you the tenant? There must be some mistake, I've just extended my contract, the flat's not available for rent, I said. I know nothing about that, I've got a viewing to do, so if you'd be so kind and let us into the flat. The couple clearly found the situation uncomfortable; embarrassment was writ large across their faces. Somehow they looked familiar. Maybe we should come back another time, the woman said. She was half a head taller than the man and quite skinny, while he looked as if he lifted weights. It hasn't been tidied, I said, but by all means take a look around and come back in three years. I thought this would get rid of them, but it was a mistake. Hardly had I opened the door than the three of them were already in the hallway, inspecting the state of the walls. They could do with a lick of paint but otherwise they're in good nick, the agent said. When they entered the kitchen the woman squealed with delight. Such a large window and that beautiful lime tree – fantastic! It'll be like having breakfast in the country. All of a sudden I saw the lime tree through different eyes; I was so used to it by now that I no longer noticed it. Would you like a coffee? I asked. Please, the woman replied. I never say no to a coffee, the man said wittily, and the agent nodded happily. I hadn't banked on that; my question had been rhetorical. They ought to have responded in the negative, with a shameful look on their faces. So on top of everything I now had to make them coffee! Ignoring me, they went into the living room. They were just as taken with the view of the park. As soon as the flat's empty it'll look quite different, I heard the agent say. I put the espresso pot on the cooker and when the coffee had brewed I took a tray with three cups into the living room. I was hoping that they wouldn't sit on the sofa, it was strewn with papers and dirty crockery, but these people were capable of anything. They took the cups from the tray and measured the room in strides, nudging aside empty boxes with their toecaps, as if they already lived here. The agent stood by the window, gazing at the park. I'd love to have somewhere with a view like this, he sighed. As if an agent couldn't have any flat they wanted. After a brief consultation the couple decided to take the flat. It's quite strong, this coffee, but it's good, the woman said. I normally drink lattes. For all I cared she could have a heart attack in this very room! Giving up such a gorgeous flat – I just don't understand it! You must have found an even better one, she blathered on. Where *had* I seen this woman before? I'd heard her voice, too. The agent gave the man a form to sign, which he did immediately, without reading it. He wasn't even given a copy. I was speechless. The agent coaxed the two of them to the door and shook my hand. Thanks for your help, you'll be hearing from us about handing over the keys. The couple waved from outside. Bye, and thanks for the coffee! I banged the door shut, turned the lock twice and stormed to the phone to call the management company. The form the agent had given the man to sign made it clear that I urgently needed something in writing. Frau Savka must send me the extension to my contract immediately.

I couldn't get through; it was permanently engaged. Tomorrow morning, then, first thing. I lay down on the sofa, all around me the rubbish tip that neither the agent nor the couple viewing my flat had remarked upon. I was in the middle of a nightmare in which a strange dog was chained to the railings on my parents' balcony. As he leaped towards the balcony door he froze, leaving him stuck in mid-air with a look of astonishment on his face – did one say 'face' for dogs, wasn't there another word for it? I didn't dare follow my first instinct, which was to untie the animal's rigid body, bring him in, wrap him in a blanket and give him a rub, because I was worried that the dog would bite me once he'd thawed out, in revenge for what had been done to him. All of a sudden the telephone rang. I had the impression it had been ringing for quite a while. I tried to get up from the sofa but fell and crawled to the phone, pushing aside empty packaging and plastic bottles. Frau Hohenembs! Highly personal. She invited me to breakfast the following morning in her apartment, for a chat. She'd lay on everything you could possibly wish for at breakfast: real hot chocolate, runny *and* whipped cream, sweet and spicy pastries, eggs prepared all ways, bacon and ham, strawberries, oranges, coffee, tea. I know you have a weakness for good food, she added at the end. I hesitated. The invitation was a chance, perhaps. I had to relearn how to deal with such situations; I'd mastered the all-you-can-eat scenario, so it must be possible for me to get through a breakfast with my dignity intact. I accepted, even though I was annoyed that once again it was she who'd called first. It made it look as if I was always waiting for something to happen. But this would be the last time! I stretched out on the floor, which compared to the sofa was agreeably flat. I laid my head on a TV magazine and fell asleep.

*

Sometimes she was obliged to spend entire mornings in a chair, her hair divided into strands and hung up on ribbons, because the weight of her plaits gave her headaches. But for her there was nothing worse than having to sit around for so long doing nothing. I'm the slave of my hair, she would often say. The hairdressing procedure used to take at least three hours. During this time I would read her Heine, or she would make conversation in Hungarian or Greek. Her hairdresser, Fanny Feifalik, who had worked styling hair in the theatre, had to show her all the hairs she had combed out on a silver platter. She received a reprimand for each one. In the end Frau Feifalik adopted the ruse of concealing the hairs that had come out with adhesive tape beneath her pinafore. Hair-washing would take place every three weeks; this had absolute priority over everything else. The date for this time-consuming operation was fixed; it occupied an entire day and everything else had to be cancelled. In this, she showed no consideration for her representative duties. Her flowing locks were coated with a mixture of raw egg yolks and cognac, which stayed on for hours. On these days she was especially ungracious. She was utterly dependent on Frau Feifalik; on the one occasion when her hairdresser was ill and a lady-in-waiting had to stand in, the whole day was ruined. Frau Feifalik exploited this dependence to have her shameful requests granted. And she performed another service that made her slightly more indispensable. She would appear as Her Majesty's doppelgänger whenever we arrived somewhere and the local dignitaries insisted on receiving my szeretett angyalom with great pomp, presenting her with useless objects, from golden keys to enormous bouquets of flowers. Her Majesty hated having attention drawn to herself in public and would send out Fanny, who was of similar build, in one of her dresses. With impeccable poise Frau Feifalik would stride through the crowd, accepting the homage of the mayors as best she could, imitating Her Majesty. In the port of Smyrna she was taken around in a barge and tributes were paid by the city dignitaries. During all of this my rose was able to wander with me through the crowds incognito. If only Frau Feifalik had been around that day in Geneva. Then the Italian would have stabbed her rather than my petal!

*

Frau Hohenembs sat opposite me in the drawing room, in the only chair with armrests; behind her stood Ida, busy arranging the mass of dark hair. Ida had squeezed herself into the white doctor's coat. Plaintive murmurings of discontent were coming from Frau Hohenembs, which were imitated by the two grey parrots in the corner. One of Frau Hohenembs's arms dangled down and stroked the huge dog lying on the floor beside her. Ida wasn't particularly skilled, maybe she didn't want to be fiddling about with hair. I could empathize with that. I find other people's hair slightly revolting. But even more revolting are other people's scalps. I don't want anything to do with something so sensitive, intimate. Frau Hohenembs had thick brown hair, you couldn't see any scalp shining through, for which I was most grateful. Eventually Ida twisted the hair into a thick plait, which she fastened at the back of Frau Hohenembs's head with long hairpins from between her pressed lips. She had the same hairstyle, although her rolled-up plait was thinner and the chestnut-brown colour streaked with grey. There was no hint of scalp on her head either. I sipped a cup of Lady Grey and took a bite of a ham roll. I'd rarely tasted a roll as good as this; it was handmade and the ham exceptionally tender. Unfortunately, the hairdressing had failed to spoil my appetite. I tried my best to avoid looking at the fully laden table and focus instead on my strategy. I was waiting for the most opportune moment to beg Frau Hohenembs to spare me from her machinations. I couldn't phrase it like that, obviously; I'd prepared something more appropriate to say, but now was the wrong moment. She was still suffering the ordeal of her morning toilette. Lucheni's head came into my mind again; I hadn't thought of it since the museum. I became boiling hot and the mouthful of ham roll felt dry against my gums and tasted unpleasantly of animal. I swallowed it without chewing and, with crumbs in my voice, asked Frau Hohenembs where the glass cylinder containing the head had been. In a closet; I didn't want it in the drawing room. But there's something quite different I need to talk to you about. The museum has acquired a new exhibit which, just like the duck presses, belongs to me. I'm awfully sorry, but we need to go back and, touch wood, retrieve this object. She said *retrieve* without any trace of irony. She'd already fixed a date, in seven days' time, for after that splendid coup with Lucheni's head she wanted to give us, Ida and me, a few days off. If it were up to her, she'd bring back the object – she didn't say what it was and I didn't ask – to where it belonged tomorrow. She understood that she couldn't expect this of us, even though her fingers were already itching. Now was the worst possible moment to execute my plan; once again I'd waited too long. Noticing my despondency, Frau Hohenembs tried to cheer me up. The media haven't yet reported on the disappearance of the duck press. Touch wood, it'll go just as smoothly as it did on the last occasion, she promised. You mustn't worry about a thing. She appeared intoxicated by the prospect of another theft, and passed a book across the table to me. Look what Ida got for me – wonderful photographs. It was a massive, thousand-page picture book with erotic photos of women from the early twentieth century. I almost knocked over a jug of milk with my outstretched arm, which sank under the weight of the book. The pictures were in black and white, and grainy, like those in the sex museum. I leafed through a few pages; the truly erotic element of the photos was the cheerfulness and levity of the models. Their bodies were unburdened, they hadn't been starved or laced up or trained in a gym or edited to make them perfect, they weren't divided into three or four types. It looked playful and harmless; I didn't know whether the models thought so too, whether they'd had fun with the photographer before, afterwards or during, or whether they'd been forced into doing it and humiliated. But there was no suggestion of coercion in the pictures. Frau Hohenembs had Ida pour her half a cup of coffee; the rest she filled with sugar and single cream. She ate two ham rolls and a curd-cheese pastry. As I looked at the coffee cup I remembered the property-management firm and how I'd planned to ring them early that morning. I'd completely forgotten, which made me furious, and I decided to complain about the behaviour of the agent working on behalf of the firm. Ida had now taken off the white coat for breakfast and she ate curd-cheese pastries, three or four of them – I wasn't really counting – with which she drank tea, or at any rate poured it down herself as you might water a pot plant after you come back from holiday. I forced myself not to eat any more and tried to persuade myself that the eating habits of the other two disgusted me. As if I hadn't done far worse myself. Frau Hohenembs stuffed down her rolls in the same way that Ida devoured her pastries; there was none of the restraint I'd seen at the picnic in the Prater. The dog, too, was now agitated; he turned his head from Ida to Frau Hohenembs and back again, but they didn't give him anything. I became sick through envy. How come these two were allowed to throw everything down their gullets while I had to make do with a single roll? I'd come a long way! Sitting there gawping in envy at two old women eating, together with this emaciated dog. Clicking my fingers and making psst noises, I tried to lure the dog over so I could stroke his head, so the two of us starving ones could band together. But he remained obstinately at Frau Hohenembs's feet, in the false and stupid hope (typical dog) that he might be allowed a morsel after all. Compared to him I had a distinct advantage: I could take as much from the table as I wanted. And this thought led me on to the next, hideous thought: just one more time. Like a poisonous vine, a complicated network of lies wound its way around this one phrase, the only purpose of which was to conceal the truth that of course it could never just be one more time.

*

At her mother's in Possenhofen it was normal for dogs to be present at mealtimes. They would sit on the duchess's lap and were permitted to eat from her plate, which meant that the servants had to keep on replacing them. The duchess's favourite dogs were white spitzes. There was a permanent mass of white on her lap and barking in the dining room. She would examine the dogs for fleas and then crush these right on the table. To either side of her the tablecloth would be littered with squashed black and brown fleas, from which seeped ruby-red dog's blood. With a silver table brush, a lackey would try to sweep the corpses onto a silver pan, but found it hard to make much headway. My kedvesem found all of this rather embarrassing. The ladies at the Viennese court gossiped viciously about it, giving them more fodder for their wicked rumours. They could not get over the fact that this country girl, unburdened by etiquette or Spanish court ceremony, had become their empress. Not only that, she far surpassed them in her natural elegance.

*

After I'd thrown up at home, panicking that it was already too late and that I wouldn't be able to get it all out – I hadn't dared try at Frau Hohenembs's, for fear of the lingering smell as well as the risk of the dog; he might have stood outside the loo door and barked or whined – I had the brilliant idea, still hanging over the toilet bowl, to go on a diet. Even better: I decided to fast. Why hadn't I thought of it before? What I needed was a transition, a cleansing ritual. Flush out body and soul – a simple calculation! And I'd lose weight too. Over the following seven days I lived off herb and fruit teas; once a day I'd drink a large glass of vegetable juice and a glass of sauerkraut juice. Not eating was so easy, and so wonderful. With great difficulty I managed to weigh myself only twice a day: mornings and evenings. I slowly restored order in the flat. In the first three days my tongue was covered in greenish-white spots, in the summer of the century my face was grey and pimply. But gradually my skin and tongue cleared up, my lymph glands went down, the worst of the toxins were out and I felt light and fresh. I was fortified for my next encounter with Frau Hohenembs; this time I'd finally tell her that she couldn't boss me about as she did Ida. On the appointed day I stood outside the museum entrance, three kilos lighter, pale, freezing and shivering, waiting for Frau Hohenembs and Ida. I was far too early; when you go on a fast you've got a lot of time on your hands. All the time you usually spend shopping, cooking, eating and washing up is now at your disposal in unlimited quantities. Just as scoffing and puking are a time waster, so fasting is a time generator. You don't know what to do with all that time. I still hadn't broken my fast; I wanted to hang on for another day or two, maybe I could lose another two kilos, which would mean I'd lost five in total. I totally failed to see that yet again I was caught in the fatal weight spiral. As soon as you've reached your weight-loss target, you set yourself another one. The ideal weight is adjusted downwards, an even number, an odd number, two more kilos then you're at forty-five instead of forty-seven; if you're forty-five, two kilos less is ideal, then you've got a cushion (a negative one!) in case you do put weight on again. If you finally get down to forty-three, you think why not forty, that's such a nice round number (in truth the number 4 already shows the bones sticking out all over the place), but then thirty-eight would be even better! Then you could put on another kilo or two without having to worry. Of course you don't put weight on again if you're thirty-eight or thirty-seven kilos (all of a sudden it starts going down as if by itself) – why should you gamble this hard-won weight loss? I finished at thirty-five kilos; I didn't manage to get any lower than that. I wasn't one of those anorexics who exhibit an extraordinary will not to eat or to eat the minutest quantities. I hated myself for not being able to achieve it, for being so undisciplined and gluttonous, lacking all self-control. Anorexics were my goddesses. I was revolting, unrestrained, perverted. They were clean, disciplined, light. I would never scale that Olympus. I couldn't maintain my thirty-five kilos. I was too weak, my willpower not strong enough, I had problems with my circulation, problems with my concentration. I was so proud when I felt dizzy, because this meant I was thin. I wanted to be absent, I wanted to disappear. All of a sudden I felt very fragile and not up to a meeting with the two of them. I considered going away again, but then I saw them approaching me with their billow-ing skirts. This time the dog was with them. As usual,

Frau Hohenembs simply began talking, without any sort of hello, while Ida shifted from one foot to the other. Perhaps her legs were aching in this heat; no real surprise given how large she was. You wait outside with the dog. Ida and I will go in and fetch the object. If you see someone following us when we come out, stop them – do something with the dog. If no one is following us then *you* follow us, but at a distance! She handed me the lead and joined the ticket queue with Ida. The dog was pulling on the lead. He wasn't wearing a muzzle. It wasn't until Ida had awkwardly squeezed through the turnstile after Frau Hohenembs – the turnstile got stuck twice and a member of the museum staff had to turn it by hand – and the two of them were out of sight that the dog relented and allowed me to walk him to a bench. Out of sight, out of mind – so this was true of dogs too. I sat down; he lay at my feet and didn't make another peep. He didn't seem to be particularly agitated. I was freezing even though I was wearing a long-sleeve jumper. My thoughts turned again to my diet and I decided that rather than fasting for just another day or two I'd keep going until the end of the week. I wasn't feeling hungry and I was convinced that I could lose another three to four kilograms, perhaps even five. After that my normal life would begin – without Frau Hohenembs and Ida! On top of that I'd be thinner. I wondered what Charlotte would think. She'd never bothered about my weight. Nor her own. For her fifty kilos were the same as sixty; figures like that were irrelevant as far as she was concerned. I was disappointed that Frau Hohenembs hadn't remarked on my weight. Another reason to delay breaking my fast. I gave a start when the dog leaped up and dashed towards the museum entrance until the lead whipped back. Frau Hohenembs and Ida were fleeing the museum, Frau Hohenembs holding a large syringe, behind them two attendants shouting something I couldn't understand. I let the dog off its leash and he rushed at one of the pursuers. The other stopped and tried to wrench the dog by its collar away from his colleague. The dog had bitten an ankle. Ida and Frau Hohenembs reached the Ringstrasse and motioned to the taxis. A pink, cab-like taxi advertising Manner wafers stopped. This had to be the most conspicuous car in the whole of Vienna. I waited till they'd driven off, then went over to the museum attendants, put the dog back on his lead and made my apologies for the animal, who'd never done anything like that before. The man who'd been bitten was sitting on the ground, cursing. He took off his shoe and sock, I could see faint teeth marks, red dots on the surface; fortunately, the dog had just held on to the ankle rather than biting it. The other man was talking on a mobile, calling the police and an ambulance. I had to stay and accompany them to the police station, where they took my statement. Thank goodness the museum employee declined to press charges; the wound wasn't particularly deep and, for him, the far greater catastrophe was the theft, which he'd been unable to prevent. It was the newest exhibit: Empress Sissi's personal cocaine syringe, which had only recently entered the museum's possession from a private collection in Switzerland. The attendant was treated on the spot. He was given a tetanus injection and a snow-white plaster. The worst thing was that the police now had my personal details and the dog's licence number with a false name I'd made up because I didn't know what he was called. They let me go once I'd signed the transcript, but with a warning that the dog would be put down by a police vet if it ever harmed anybody again. This would be at my cost, with a hefty fine to boot.

I delivered the dog back to Frau Hohenembs and went home. The couple who'd viewed my flat were standing outside the door. I was at the far end of the corridor. But it was too late to turn around; they'd already seen me and were slowly coming in my direction. I didn't move. I still hadn't got through to the property-management company. They both put an arm around my shoulder and pushed me to the front door. They smelled of pub and sweat, of cold smoke. Their leather-jacketed arms lay heavily on my shoulders. Come on, open up. The man slammed the door behind us; the woman kept her arm around my shoulder. She was a head taller than me and quite strong, despite being so lanky. She directed me into the living room and pushed me onto the sofa. What do you want? I asked. The flat's not available, I've already told you that. The woman sat down beside me, her right thigh was touching my left. The man wandered up and down, picking up newspapers and items of laundry like Frau Hohenembs over a week earlier, dropping them again, scraping at the floor with his foot as if trying to rub away an invisible mark, then he opened his mouth and said, Listen, we're only interested in the flat. You're going to be out by next Tuesday; you can take whatever you like of your things. We'll come on Tuesday and get the keys. If you don't hand them over willingly... we'll have to handcuff you. He rubbed a wrist. His leather jacket tautened at the shoulders. The woman put an arm around my waist; she held me so tightly that I could feel my ribs. I gasped for air noisily, I couldn't help it. It'll get tighter, she said. When they'd left I rang the property-management company. This time I got through. They didn't know anything about the conversation with a Frau Savka, there was no employee with that name working there, I must be mistaken. And unless I could show them something in writing any extension to my contract would not be legally binding. My contract was running out, they said, I hadn't bothered to extend it and consequently the flat was being let out to another party.

BOOK TWO

I'm living with Frau Hohenembs now. She's given me a small room in her apartment, a closet really, but it's not that tiny; it's even bigger than Ida's. It's the room where Lucheni's head used to be stored. I kitted it out with my furniture. I've got my bed and my sofa, my desk with the computer and my office chair. For the few items of clothing I possess I use one of Frau Hohenembs's old cupboards. Ida cleared it out for me and gave it the once-over with a foul-smelling cleanser. It took almost a fortnight for the revolting pong to disappear. In the apartment Ida wears the white coat during the day. Sometimes she forgets to take it off when we sit down to eat; Frau Hohenembs raps her knuckles on the table and shouts, Ida! Take off the coat! Then she'll unbutton and remove it, only to have to put it on again five minutes later because Frau Hohenembs has finished her food so quickly, and Ida has to clear the table. I've got a few books here and a CD player. It's only temporary. Frau Hohenembs has promised me a new apartment. An acquaintance of hers, Baron Wachtel, is close to death.

The baron is ninety-five and bedridden, and, sooner or later, the apartment will become free. It's more than 200 square metres, with a terrace and a view of the city. She's going to sign the apartment over to me; she has no use for it herself. On the first evening Frau Hohenembs took me into her bedroom, where there was a large set of scales made from white-painted cast iron with golden edges, manufactured by the firm F. Russ in the nineteenth century; some doctors and chemists still use museum pieces like that. I was to get on the scales. Ida jotted down my weight, forty-nine kilograms, in a notebook dedicated to this very purpose. Ida was weighed too and in the end Frau Hohenembs got on. She pushed the sliding weight back and forth a number of times, muttering unintelligibly. She weighed forty-nine kilos too, even though she's a good fifteen centimetres taller than me. There was a notebook each for the two of them as well, in which Ida carefully entered the figures. Frau Hohenembs said nothing about my weight, but she shook her head disapprovingly at Ida's. If you go on like that, she said, it's not going to end well. Show me your food diary. Ida handed over a well-thumbed notebook that she'd pulled from her dress. Frau Hohenembs flicked through it; she was not happy. I think you only note down half of what you eat – how else could you be so fat? Ida lowered her gaze. She probably didn't even write down half of it. She repeats this ritual every evening. It reminds me of my grandfather, who spent years producing daily weight graphs. If the line rose too steeply upwards because he had *sinned*, he would instruct my grandmother to arrange a day of just potatoes or polenta, which she would be forced to join him in. She herself developed gastric ulcers because, for months on end when she was forty, she drank freshly squeezed lemon juice on an empty stomach. After four pregnancies even she became unhappy with her figure. My grandfather would always ask me about my weight too, whistling through his teeth and looking aghast when I told him how many kilos, as if I'd said 150 rather than fifty-five. Strange that a grandfather should be interested in his granddaughter's weight. For years he tormented me with comments about my appearance. Saying I was heavier than my mother, that I had footballer's calves, fat upper arms and that I was *really well stacked*, whereas he'd describe my mother (his daughter) as *beautifully slim* and then as *too thin*. But the two of us weren't that different. He didn't like my eating habits either. I shouldn't mash my potatoes in the sauce, why on earth did I eat the meat first, then the mashed potatoes at the end, if I wanted seconds I ought to take more of everything rather than just potatoes, I should eat my ice cream more quickly before it all melted, I'd soon be able to dip my bread in it, was I waiting for the ice cream and whipped cream to slosh together into a *soup*? I never ate fast enough, *the mill grinds slowly*, or, if I left something on my plate, then *your eyes are bigger than your belly*. Although the others berated him, *Leave her alone, she can eat how she likes*, he put me off my lunch. There was nothing nicer than being able to warm up my own food and sit on my own in front of the television at my grandparents' dining table, or going outside in summer to my secret places – the box store or the tree house – to eat there, or alone in the empty kitchen. Then Grandfather's control ceased. I could mash and mix my food to my heart's content and eat as slowly as I liked. I could balance the plate on my thighs. The plate could fall on the floor. I could eat it all up or chuck half away. It was absolute freedom and the opposite of what my mother had grown up with. As a child, if she didn't finish her plate she'd be made to sit for hours on her own in the dining room with her congealed leftovers. Her grandmother, who cooked for the family, forced her to. The coal would have burned down in the dining room, nobody would have put more on and the stove would have gone out. The room would be as cold as the lump of food on the plate. Her grandmother's cooking was fatty and gooey. She sweated vegetables in flour and lard. No fat, gristle or bone was ever removed from the meat. If you got a tendon in your mouth you were never allowed to spit it out: *We'd have been grateful for that in the war.* If my mother saw it in time and cut it off the meat, she could pass it over to her grandfather, who would cheerfully cry, *You don't know what you're missing!*, make a big show of putting it in his mouth and pull a face as if savouring a rare delicacy. If, in spite of all her caution, my mother got a tendon in her mouth, she'd try to swallow it, but the tendon would often stick in her throat and she'd start retching and have to run into the kitchen and spit it out into the bin. Even if she did manage to swallow the tendon she'd be filled with such horror at the thought of that squidgy thing making its way down her that she'd have to stop eating there and then. At some point in the afternoon the maid would liberate my mother from the nauseating mass she was obstinately sitting in front of. She would be crying tears of fury and hatred. The maid would tip the leftovers into the bucket of slops reserved for the pig, and give her an apple. In the mornings the dog scratches at the door. When I let him in he looks around, wrinkles his dog nose, as if looking for something, and leaves the room. I think he's searching for Lucheni's head, which he used to bark at around this time of day. But he's incorrigible; he keeps trying. Ida wasn't pleased when I moved in. She's not getting my room! she griped at Frau Hohenembs. The two parrots in the corner imitated her: She's not getting my room! She's not getting my room! Ida hurled an embroidered cushion in their direction, which knocked the cage, fell to the floor and was dragged off by the dog. The startled parrots flew into the air, then settled back on their perch and, aggrieved, buried their beaks in their feathers. Frau Hohenembs didn't bat an eyelid. I still don't know what the dog's name is, maybe Lucheni. I've put into storage the rest of my things that there isn't room for here. It doesn't cost much. I wasn't going to leave those crooks who've stolen my flat so much as a cup. I've tried to ring Charlotte on a number of occasions; the first few times it was engaged or I was put straight through to voicemail. Eventually I was told the number didn't exist any more. I tried directory enquiries – there was no phone number listed for her. I rang the number a few more times; I hadn't been misdialling, sadly; Charlotte was unobtainable.

*

She developed an almost maternal attentiveness to tame my gluttony. She was forever telling me how harmful it was to eat so much. My édes szeretett angyalom was permanently concerned that I would get too big and she appeared appalled by my weight; I was ordered onto the scales regularly. But I always had a good appetite and, whatever my personal circumstances, food was a tonic for me. I was unable to go without it, even if it was not always of the highest quality – the fact that I was not particularly choosy was what astonished her most. Especially for my aggravating headaches, food proved a reliable remedy.

*

My mornings are generally free, then at two p.m. we have lunch together, prepared by Ida. There's always lots of meat and few vegetables, and barely a salad leaf in sight. In the afternoons we take a long walk in the Vienna Woods or the meadows of the Prater. A Greek teacher comes three mornings a week for conversation with Frau Hohenembs. He's short, a little stunted, and he worships Frau Hohenembs like a Greek goddess. She bosses him around, but he puts up with everything. He never stays for lunch, although there's plenty to go around; Ida always cooks too much. I get the feeling that each time the lesson is over he's hoping for an invitation from Frau Hohenembs. He'll gaze dreamily at the lunch table, which by then Ida has laboriously set for three, sticking his large nose into the air. Mmmm, he'll say, that smells good. What delicacies are on the menu today? When nobody answers him he shuffles indolently towards the hall, casting several longing glances back at the table. Once out of the door he slams it shut behind him, his only protest against his poor treatment, and something he only dares to do because he's out of reach. I once spoke to Frau Hohenembs about it, but she didn't give me an answer. And yet it would be a nice change to have someone different at the table. Frau Hohenembs picks at her food, pushing pieces of meat and potatoes from one side of the plate to the other until everything's cold. She eats a little of the meat and leaves the rest. Or she eats nothing at all, just drinking raw spiced meat juice or whisked salted egg whites, orange juice if I'm lucky, a glass of milk if I'm not. As I find white dairy products nauseating, I can barely look if anyone's having them. As a child I could have earned money drinking milk, for my parents offered me five schillings for each glass, but in spite of my childish desire for money I couldn't get it down me. The grainy streaks of white that run slowly and viscously down the inside of the glass make my stomach turn, with buttermilk being the most repugnant of all. Only at breakfast does Frau Hohenembs eat at a normal speed, choosing things that don't put me off my food. Sometimes, however, Ida has to make British porridge, which I detest as much as milk. *It keeps you going*, Frau Hohenembs affirms with all seriousness when she sees my face; this is what she kept hearing in Britain. Ida, on the other hand, keeps wolfing it down like there's no tomorrow, and when Frau Hohenembs is on liquids only, her pace becomes even more frenzied for fear that Frau Hohenembs could finish at any moment. Ida has the repulsive habit of continuing to chew on her food for an hour or two if she thinks no one's watching. She'll retch up a bite back into her mouth, chew on it, then swallow it again. I imagine it comes from the need to eat so quickly at the table, because otherwise she never gets enough. On the occasions when Frau Hohenembs catches her doing this she'll scream, Ida! You're doing your revolting thing again – stop it at once! Ida will turn away and swallow guiltily, but the moment she's certain that she's no longer under close scrutiny she'll start again. It reminds me of my most embarrassing experience. It's so embarrassing I can hardly bear to remind myself; not even Charlotte knows. What would Frau Hohenembs say? Once when I'd cooked and eaten spaghetti with sauce, I felt I hadn't had enough; I was hungry for more, no matter what it was. But there was nothing else to eat, so I vomited onto my empty plate and had another go at the puked-up spaghetti, now in smaller bits. The actual eating of it wasn't the worst, as I couldn't taste any gastric acid and it looked like tinned spaghetti for little children. But afterwards, when I'd thrown up a second time, now in the loo, I was so ashamed that I got ill and couldn't eat again for days. Later I found out that, in Catholic and state homes for children, one of the favourite punishments in the 1950s and 60s, and even into the 70s, was to make children sit in front of their plates until everything was eaten up, and if they vomited in disgust, which was not a rare occurrence because the food in those institutions was often inedible, they had to eat up what was left on their plate *and* the sick. Come what may, the plate had to be empty. I was never forced to eat up every last morsel – my mother was still haunted by all those plates with ice-cold food – I did it willingly. In spite of this, full of self-pity, I wallowed in the image of the soup bowl I'd thrown up into twenty years ago. A white soup bowl, an everyday bowl, not from a posh dinner service. The bowl was on the stained, smooth kitchen table, together with all those things that accumulate on kitchen tables: salt cellar, pepper mill, used napkins, sugar bowl, newspapers, brochures, biros, notepad, instruction leaflets for medicines, crumbs. Crying and sobbing, perhaps even gagging – the scene became ever more dramatic in my memory – I spooned up the sick. I find myself increasingly getting carried away by Ida and so start eating more than I actually want to, which puts me into great difficulty. It's very hard for me to puke here: the lavatory is right next to Frau Hohenembs's bedroom. I can't sneak off unnoticed, as you have to go through the drawing room and Frau Hohenembs's bedroom, a disagreeable undertaking, particularly at night. The parrots, whose cage is covered with a blanket, must not be woken, otherwise they'll get ill. And then there's the dog, who, when he's not asleep, tends to follow you wherever you go. Frau Hohenembs says I'm allowed to use the loo (as is Ida) whenever I like. If she's not in her bedroom I'm always worried she might burst in at any moment, for you can't lock the loo door; if she *is* there I feel like an annoying intruder. At night I never know if Frau Hohenembs is pretending to be asleep and listening to the sounds I make, or whether she really can't hear anything at all, which is what you'd think from the regular rattle of her breathing. If Ida's in the loo, which you can tell by the strip of light beneath the door, I return to my room, listen for her to come back, then enter Frau Hohenembs's bedroom again; she seems oblivious to all this coming and going, but I don't trust her. Sometimes I'll wait more than half an hour, but Ida still won't have come back. Then I have to check whether she really is in the loo or if she's just forgotten to turn out the light. It's perfectly possible, of course, that Ida deliberately keeps the light on to rob me of sleep. Few words are spoken at the table – Ida hasn't got time to speak because her mouth is permanently full and Frau

Hohenembs is lost in her thoughts. Sometimes she stops eating unexpectedly and writes poetry in a black notebook. If she's in a particularly good mood she'll read out selected verses and we have to give our opinion. Ida marvels at these outpourings; I maintain that I know nothing about poetry. Her verses are vulgar doggerel; only seldom is there the odd bite or even humour. They bear witness to her contempt for everyone. What's more, she claims Heine as her inspiration. These poems are the only thing she pens herself; everything else is dictated to Ida, or, more frequently now, me. Like Ida, I have to have a notebook on me at all times. Mostly it's shopping lists or instructions for small tasks we'll carry out later. Frau Hohenembs wanted me to keep a food diary like Ida, but I refused. Maybe you'll reconsider, she said, handing me an A5 hardback writing book – Italian, with thick colourful paper inside and small images on the cover. It really is a great help. I've kept umpteen food diaries in my life; I've added up millions of calories, and subtracted, divided and multiplied, all of it useless. It never meant I weighed one gram more or less. All it did was reinforce my obsession with food, which fills every cell of my body anyway. My thoughts focus only on the next meal, how I can compensate for the last meal with the next one (best to skip it altogether), what I'm not going to eat any more or, caught up in the delirium, all the things that are going to be bought on the next shopping trip. Ida keeps Frau Hohenembs's food diary. She falsifies her own unashamedly. It's not just that she notes less than she's eaten, as Frau Hohenembs rightly suspects, but she also puts down other things like fruit and vegetables, things she gives a wide berth, except in processed forms such as jam and pickles. In light of the unfavourable loo situation, I've had to reinstate my old screw-top jar system that I used as a little girl. I vomit in my bedroom into large jars I hide in the cupboard or behind the bookshelves. In the past these jars were my emergency puking vessels; plastic bags were no good because the smell leaked out. From the jars I was able to gauge my weakness, this unappetizing weakness that manifests itself as the contents of a jar in muted, dirty colours and in various layers. The worst is when I want to puke and there isn't an empty jar, which is a regular occurrence. I haven't collected that many jars as it isn't easy to pinch them unobserved from Ida's kitchen. When I was a girl these jars would remain in my bedroom for weeks, fermenting away. Sometimes the lid would pop off and the jars explode. Which meant the puke would fly all over books or my clothes. Or I'd vomit into empty 500-gram yoghurt pots, which I would seal with aluminium foil and plastic bands, then hide in the loft under dusty beams. I've no idea what happened to those pots. They're probably still there today, empty and mouldy, because mice and rats will have gobbled up the contents. If I don't find a way of emptying out these jars without being seen, they'll leak and emit a God-awful stench. I can only empty them if I'm alone in the apartment and that's happened just twice. Barely had I emptied the jars down the loo, washed them in the kitchen and hidden them in my room again than the two of them were back and the dog was snuffling around me interestedly. I can't throw the jars away; I'd have to get new ones and that would arouse too much suspicion, as Ida uses the empty jars for making jam and pickling peppers. I could buy some, but I can't smuggle them into the apartment unnoticed; I have to ring the bell when I come home. Frau Hohenembs promised me a key when I first came here; Ida was instructed to get some cut for the entrance downstairs and the door to the apartment, but she keeps procrastinating – the key-cutter is on holiday or he's changed his opening hours, then she doesn't have any time or she can't find her own key, etc. How am I supposed to justify buying a bag full of clanking jars? Ida would assume they were for her preserves. If I don't have any opportunity to throw up in the apartment I go to the park just down the road, wait till there's no one about, then puke behind a hedge. I avoid looking up at my old flat. Sometimes I notice inadvertently that the windows are open or closed, or the blinds are down. Then I quickly turn my head and leave the park. Or I go to the loo in an ice-cream parlour. As cover I'll buy an ice cream afterwards, which I'll throw away outside before I can succumb to the temptation of eating it. Unfortunately, *that* smell is hanging in my room again. In the past this sour stench pervaded my bedroom, I was permanently surrounded by it, I lived in it. My mother and father would grimace whenever they entered my room. They didn't have to say anything; I could tell from their faces that they could smell it when I came out of the loo or bathroom, or back from a walk that I'd taken to throw up behind a bush. The pungent smell clung to my body. It stuck to my clothes, my hair; it must have been literally emanating from me. The stench of fermented sick will follow me all my life. I can smell it spontaneously in the most unlikely places. All I have to do is see a skinny girl somewhere – and I see them everywhere; they spring from the ground like scrawny mushrooms – and the smell is back in my nostrils. On Saturday afternoons we always go to a betting café. Frau Hohenembs watches dog and horse racing and places complex wagers. Sometimes Ida will advise her against a bet, but this doesn't stop her from placing it. Mostly Ida is proved right. Although Frau Hohenembs never misses a race and must know all the animals by now, her gambling success is limited. Occasionally, I'll put money on a horse whose name I like, or on a greyhound with a particularly long fringe or whose eyes look noticeably sad. I have even less luck than Frau Hohenembs; I've never won a single race. During the races Frau Hohenembs will torment us with tales from the time when she rode herself; she used to be one of the best hunt riders in the whole of Europe, she claims. Only a few men could keep pace with her, and they'd stay close by, following her like dolphins do a ship. Her escapades in Hungary and England, and later in Ireland, were legendary; the Queen of the Hunt, the British gazettes used to call her. When half of the riders had been thrown into ditches and had to shoot their horses because they had broken their legs or their bellies were gashed open, she'd long since negotiated all the obstacles. And this in the uncomfortable ladies' saddle she used for official hunts, and in uncomfortable skirts. If she rode alone, or with her niece, she used a man's saddle and wore men's clothes. That was true happiness. You know! She was worshipped by all the well-known riders, both in Hungary and in Britain; everywhere she had the world at her feet. The Irish were particularly attached to her, she said, they still talk about her there to this day. She forged a place in the Irish consciousness as a mysterious fairy on horseback around whom legends grew. The sun and wind turned her the colour of a hare; her face was covered in freckles. The shuddering and foaming horses, the riders in red, the children on ponies and the English hounds with brown patches. The green fields. You don't get that sort of green over here, she said. And English parkland, Irish forests. Oh, those were the days. Taking after her father, she also used to perform artistic riding tricks in the circus arenas she had built; her trainer was the famous circus rider Elise Renz. And – just imagine this – everything came to an end from one day to the next. All of a sudden, and for no reason, I lost my courage. I, who scorned every danger, now saw it lurking behind every bush, and I could not get these fearful visions out of my head! And riding is so good for the figure; even Flaubert said that. This is how she brags during those long Saturday afternoons in the gloomy, air-conditioned betting café. They know us here; the waiter automatically brings us two raspberry sodas (for Ida and me) and a lemon soda (for Frau Hohenembs). After the betting café we visit a confectioner's. We have to make our way right across the city, because this particular confectioner's is the solitary one in Vienna that makes violet ice cream according to an old Trieste recipe – the only ice cream Frau Hohenembs eats. It has a faintly euphoric effect. We eat three large portions and Frau Hohenembs orders another litre to take home. We mustn't get any more as it spoils after a couple of days in the freezer compartment. Ida and I sit intoxicated next to each other on the tram. Frau Hohenembs, who as a matter of principle stands in the tram, looks out of the window giggling, with a hand to her mouth. Ida brings her ice cream back up into her mouth, probably dreaming of Corfu. In her youth she must have got caught up in something which Frau Hohenembs is now shamelessly exploiting. I'm only going to spend a short time here, then I'll go and she won't be able to stop me. When that Baron Wachtel dies at the very latest. Then she'll have to give me the flat. I'm certain she lied that time on the phone when she said she knew how she could keep herself and Ida out of the affair. If I were to tip off the police, the two of them would be in quite a bit of hot water. But they would implicate me. So I've got to sit it out. She gives me a little pocket money; my account is blocked. My only outgoings are for storage and what I spend in secret on food. I get by, but only just, and only because I changed up the collection of coins I found in the hall cupboard. They must have been the coins Frau Hohenembs was talking about when we were in the Prater. The first and only money she had ever earned. The coin album looked so dusty and forgotten that I hoped its disappearance would pass unnoticed. And it has, so far at least. I've had to break my fast. Eating then vomiting is the only thing that gives me a connection to my past. The palais of the Ringstrasse pass by the windows of the tram, these massive, grand buildings from the late nineteenth century. A melancholic evening is looming. When the effect of the violet ice cream wears off, Ida will administer Frau Hohenembs a dose of cocaine with the syringe from the museum – for medicinal purposes, as she claims. Then Ida will reach for her schnapps glass and I will consume the two 500-gram bags of bittersweet chocolate wafers that I've been hoarding. The parrots will be covered and the dog will sleep.

*

My szeretett angyalom tried everything to maintain her figure. All her life my angel was on the hunt for the ideal slimming regime. She tried seawater, chalybeate baths, hay baths, sweating and fasting treatments, massages, sun waves, sand and steam baths. Not to mention the various diets: oranges, grapes, milk, meat juice and many more. She had two bathing cabins built at the Villa Hermes, one for her and one for Katharina Schratt, the emperor's lady friend, in which the two of them would be 'roasted or burned', as the horrified emperor feared. All this just to expedite the definitive fat removal. He found it all utter nonsense and he was pleased that the 'medical experiments', as he called these treatments, did not cause either woman particular harm. He acted as the messenger between her and Katharina Schratt, for my petal was absorbed by every kilo and gram that the emperor's lady friend lost, while he fretted that she would become too slim and that the empress would drag her into a disastrous routine of starvation. His lady friend never lasted very long, however; she could not keep up with my slim dove. All her life she remained a buxom woman whose corsets burst at the seams.

*

A few days ago Ida had to teach me how to give Frau Hohenembs her injection. Frau Hohenembs doesn't want Ida to inject her any more as she says she's got the shakes, which I haven't noticed. Ida defended herself, insisting she could give the injections in her sleep, no matter how much she trembled. But it was useless. She had to show me and I had to try. My first attempt caused chaos. I aimed for the vein in Frau Hohenembs's arm that Ida had strapped, but I was too cautious: the needle slipped and blood flowed from the crook of her arm. The shock made me squeeze all the cocaine out of the needle; it squirted onto the floor and the dog licked up every drop. Gritting her teeth, Frau Hohenembs ordered Ida to refill the syringe. Ida strapped the other arm. This time I succeeded in getting the needle into the vein, but I forgot to squeeze out the liquid. Come on! Frau Hohenembs cried. She'll never get it! Ida growled. Come on! the parrots chorused. I pressed down the plunger and Frau Hohenembs got her cocaine. I took out the needle too brutally, tearing off a bit of pale skin. Are you mad? Frau Hohenembs screamed. I hadn't put any cotton wool on the spot where the needle had gone in, which meant that a blue bruise soon formed, even though Ida had been waiting with a whole bag of sterilized cotton wool. It's what you wanted, Ida grumbled at Frau Hohenembs as she undid the elastic band from the thin arm and put a plaster on both punctures. She'll soon learn, Frau Hohenembs said. You weren't any better first time round. She pushed down her sleeves and held her arms out to Ida so they could be buttoned up. I was still holding the syringe. It seemed far too chunky for a human being. Ida told me to clean the needle and put the syringe back into its case. Frau Hohenembs noticed that there was a spot of blood on my T-shirt and she suggested that in the daytime I wear a housecoat like Ida; it would be more practical. I declined, saying it wasn't necessary. Who's paying for the washing powder? Frau Hohenembs spat out. Me, of course, me, me, me! The fine lady gets filthy and I'm left paying for the washing powder because the fine lady's far too grand for a housecoat! I was nonplussed. This was the first time she'd shouted at me. She'd said nothing about the spilled cocaine, but now this outburst about a bit of washing powder. Housecoat, housecoat, came the squawks from the corner of the parrots' cage and the dog started barking and racing like crazy around the table; the cocaine was taking effect. I'll pay for the washing powder myself, then, I replied. I'm not wearing a housecoat. Ida whistled through her teeth. Her round face looked relaxed and peaceful; she was probably happy to remain the only one in a housecoat. Go and buy some now, then, Frau Hohenembs said, before turning around and retiring to her bedroom. The dog followed her, his hair on end. I bought the largest box of washing powder I could find, making use of the opportunity to get some food for my secret eating sessions. When I returned Ida opened the door. What lovely things have you bought? she asked nosily. Handing her the box of washing powder, I asked when I was finally going to get my own keys. The locksmith's on holiday, she said cheekily. It had been the summer holidays only two weeks ago. There must be other locksmiths, I argued. I'm not going all the way across town just for you, she exclaimed. Give me the keys, I don't mind going across town. Well I never, she groaned. That's all I need! Me sitting here without any keys! She stuffed the bunch of keys, which usually sat in the lock, into her housecoat and went off with the washing powder. I unpacked the food in my room and stacked it in the chest. I moved the packets about like building blocks, rearranging them over and over again, so that everything was in the right place, as if I wasn't going to eat things in a random way next time.

*

When we were travelling I was forever having to copy menus and send them to the emperor. The two of them would exchange the details of every dinner they took apart; the emperor, in particular, was interested in the dishes served in other places. He was a great eater; his appetite was never diminished by any misfortune, no matter how tragic. I enjoyed copying these lists; it gave me the pleasure of at least imagining the meals my édes lelkem had eaten. I also kept diaries for her; every day her weight had to be written down, and during her diets and cures I had to make a note of everything she ate and drank. She was incredibly pedantic in this regard.

*

Our trip to the Habsburg furniture collection yielded a commemorative screen mounted with photographs and pictures of important events in the life of Empress Elisabeth. It came from the bequest of one of the empress's granddaughters, Erzsi, who became known as the Red Duchess, having married a socialist. Frau Hohenembs was beside herself when she saw the piece; she'd been totally unaware of its existence. She walked around the screen, squealing with delight whenever she spotted something of interest. Although many of the photographs were in her drawing room, she refused to leave the museum without the screen. She dropped her original plan to sabotage the special exhibition on the *Sissi* films – or to have me and Ida sabotage it. The exhibition consisted of several rooms with original furniture from Sissi's childhood bedroom, which had later been used for the set of the *Sissi* films. A dress or two, a studio light, director's chair with the director's name, punctuated by film posters with Romy Schneider and Karlheinz Böhm, charts with Romy Schneider's filmography, photos of her mother, Magda Schneider, and father, Wolf Albach-Retty. Three projectors showed loops from each of the three *Sissi* films in different languages. The first scene was in Schönbrunn Palace, where the newly married Sissi brings her Franzl a bunch of roses and complains that he spends all his time working at his desk, rather than looking after his young wife. Franzl is embarrassed and delighted by the flowers, but there's nothing he can do because the documents are piling up and the servants keep carting in more. The second excerpt showed Sissi's mother-in-law instructing a lady-in-waiting in guttural Spanish to take Sissi's diary from the desk and give it to her, while in the third scene Sissi and Franzl were sitting on their thrones, hectically discussing something important in perfect Italian. The idea was for us to throw sand into the projectors and deface the posters. Ida had sand and fluorescent markers in her new rucksack. We're no match for these *Sissi* films and Romy Schneider's fresh and rosy face, Frau Hohenembs said. And you had to give the actress credit for distancing herself from these kitsch productions later on and moving to revolutionary France – of all places – where she played completely different roles. She was still young and under the influence of her mother; it's easy to do things you regret afterwards. How could she have rebelled? Born into an acting family that, from early childhood, prescribed for her parts she had to play. There were parallels with the empress. For a young duchess, destined to marry into one of the royal houses of Europe, an emperor was a real stroke of luck, especially a young, handsome one to whom she was related. She could have come off far worse, like her sisters. A cancelled engagement to King Ludwig of Bavaria, who with his theatrical disposition was thoroughly unsuited to his position; an impotent husband; expulsion from the Kingdom of the Two Sicilies; a child out of wedlock; the premature death of a husband. She was spared all of this. Later, Frau Hohenembs continued, she escaped all her burdensome representational duties and, for a monarch of her time, carved out an unusually independent life beyond the court ceremonial, unconcerned with what the flunkeys and people thought, just as Romy Schneider broke free from her mother at some point, stopped worrying about the opinions of her entourage and the public, and turned down another, long-planned, film in the series. One had to acknowledge this, and her

unconventional beauty spoke in her favour too. The
empress didn't conform to the ideal of beauty of her
era either, and yet she was indisputably a *style icon*, as
people say today, just as Romy Schneider is an icon for
modern sapphics. So Romy Schneider was spared and
we had to improvise. As we were the only visitors in
the museum, Ida and I managed to fold shut the screen
unimpeded and remove it from the exhibition rooms. No
alarm was triggered. Frau Hohenembs showed the ticket
lady a piece of paper and said the screen's wood needed
restoring, upon which the lady picked up the phone and
talked to someone who evidently gave his assent. Frau
Hohenembs signed a form that the ticket lady had filled
out. She also bought a box set of the three *Sissi* films
that was still on special offer and a packet of three Sissi
pictures, and – everything perfectly above board – we
carried the screen out of the museum. Now it's standing beside Frau Hohenembs's bed, which has led to a
substantial improvement in the night-time loo situation.

*

*At the great Vienna World Exposition, which was years
in the preparation and lasted six months, she was conspicuous by her absence. No small number of members
of Europe's royal houses were bitterly disappointed,
as they had come just to see her. Round the clock the
entire imperial family were busy with representational
duties, with the 'hustle and bustle'. My kedvesem kept*

coming up with excuses, such as Holy Week or a variety of indispositions, and rarely let herself be 'thrust into the fray'. When the entire city was unsettled by news of a cholera outbreak, this played into her hands. She interrupted her summer holiday in Payerbach only for the Shah of Persia, for he threatened not to leave until he had been personally introduced to my petal, and he unashamedly took over the quarters put at his disposal in Laxenburg. 'The Centre of the Universe' was a difficult guest indeed. Cooking stoves, butcher's blocks and fire pits for the enormous smoking pipes had to be installed in his apartments; lambs had to be slaughtered and roasted before his eyes, naturally causing damage to the parquet floors. He had his own chicken house erected, for he personally used to slaughter three of the birds at sunrise. He would often turn up hours late to gala dinners and openings, because his astrologist had advised him against the fixed schedule on account of unfavourable constellations, recommending a different time instead. And when he finally was able to lay his eyes upon her, his joy was so great that, in front of everyone present, he cried, Ah, qu'elle est belle! To the relief of us all, he was gracious enough to leave the following day.

*

A few days after our visit to the Habsburg furniture collection Frau Hohenembs handed me a flyer for a summer ball. All Sissi fans were requested to appear in an evening gown based on a historic Sissi dress. The theme of the ball was *Sissi for a Night*. Around midnight a vote would take place to elect Miss Sissi 2007. The winner would receive her weight in original Viennese violet pralines. We're going to win those pralines, Frau Hohenembs giggled, with a hand to her mouth. Then she frowned and said grimly, Besides, we have to stop one of those bogus Sissis from winning. I can picture exactly how tasteless these women are going to look when they turn up. I'm too old, unfortunately, but you could do it. As usual she did not ask for my opinion. She began rummaging through her wardrobe and actually found a dress for me, which I was to wear as Empress Sissi. A white ball gown, spangled with golden stars, and a see-through tulle sash. She let me try it on there and then; it didn't fit and was too long in any case. How short you are, Frau Hohenembs exclaimed, as if only noticing this for the first time, then she said, There's no time left to slim. Ida will let it out a bit at the waist and take it up at the bottom. A corset would be a waste of time; you need to be laced into one for years to get a decent waist. She delved further into her chest and pulled out a pair of cream-coloured shoes of iridescent satin with curved heels. The parrots shuffled up and down their perches, observing me with their drawing-pin eyes, but kept their traps shut. That same afternoon Ida made the alterations to the dress, while my feet swelled up inside the shoes. Ida cursed me until the dress finally fitted. I

swore to myself that I would lose weight, even if Frau
Hohenembs thought it was too late. It was never too late;
a kilo or two was always possible, especially from the
tummy. I thought of the thirty-five kilos I'd once been
and knew that I could reach that weight again any time
I wanted to. But I didn't want to; I was sensible. I forced
myself to tolerate all the flesh and fat on my bones. It
was healthier to weigh fifty kilos instead of thirty-five.
I knew this, but I didn't feel it. My body didn't feel it.
All it felt was lead weights pressing it down. The idea
of the pralines weighed down on me too; the thought
of having fifty kilos of chocolate in the apartment was
too much, even for me. That is not the sort of stock
you want. Ida had to adjust the seam of the puff sleeves
too, for they were cutting into my arms. They were still
too narrow afterwards, but Ida refused to alter them
again. She went into the kitchen, leaving me there in
a dress I couldn't get out of on my own. I sat carefully on a chair and stopped the dog sniffing beneath
the flounced-skirt part. Frau Hohenembs came in and
shooed him away. What are you doing sitting there and
creasing that dress? That's not why I had it altered for
you! I'm waiting for Ida; I can't take it off on my own,
I replied. Ida! she called. Help her out of the dress,
quickly, quickly! Chewing on something, Ida shuffled
into the drawing room and helped me peel off the dress.
She smelled of bacon – that surely wouldn't be jotted
down in her notebook. There isn't a minute's peace in
this household, she griped, tugging at the material to

pull it over my head. The dress and the shoes were put back in the wardrobe. From then until the ball – it was only two days – I took a leaf out of Frau Hohenembs's book and got by on liquids. Ida indulged her appetite to the full. On the afternoon of the big event I could only take a quick shower as Frau Hohenembs and Ida occupied the bathroom together for hours. Both of them wore black silk dresses. I was looking forward to the ball and could barely wait to be among people again. I wanted to dance, drink, maybe snog someone, forget everything. Maybe I'd bump into Charlotte, I thought in a moment of madness. She wouldn't dream of going to an event like that. I'd never have had the idea myself to enter a Sissi-lookalike competition. Their influence on me had been so strong that I was now keen to do it of my own volition and I could already picture myself as the queen of the ball. I was thinking of escape and hoping that someone – Charlotte! – would abduct and liberate me from Frau Hohenembs. With Ida's help, I put on the gown and then had to sit down at the dressing table in Frau Hohenembs's bedroom so Ida could arrange my hair. She brushed with rough strokes and tied two simple plaits that hung down to the left and right. My hair was not long enough for any complicated coils around the head of the sort you could see in the copies of Sissi's photos. Frau Hohenembs took a handful of stars set with rhinestones from a box and attached them to my plaits. She took a step back, examined her work. Fantastic, the pralines are ours, she exclaimed, What do you say, Ida? Ida nodded. No jewellery and no make-up, I think, Frau Hohenembs said. That way she'll stand out from all those kitsch Sissis. The empress never wore make-up and she had little time for jewellery either. I was surprised myself; although my hanging plaits didn't match Sissi's classic hairstyle – the fashion of the time was evidently for hair tied up – the overall look was remarkably similar. This was chiefly down to the dress and the rhinestone stars, but I also had the same hair colour and was just as pale as the Sissi in the pictures, and this in summer.

*

On one occasion she had the newest circus attraction in Buda brought to Gödöllő: two Negro girls, fused at birth. The emperor was so horrified he wouldn't even look at them. Another time a travelling entertainer arrived with a dancing bear during her summer holiday. Her partiality to such attractions was known far and wide, encouraging all manner of characters to try their luck. We had great fun with the bear, which she fed, stroked and made jump into a lake. In spite of her desperate pleas to the emperor he refused to buy it for her – he found these sorts of sensations unsettling. In Merano she had the giantess Eugénie, who weighed 200 kilograms and who was on display in a show booth, collected by carriage and taken to her residence for inspection. In Verona she visited the Missionary Institute for Negroland, a school

where poor Negroes who had been bought out of slavery
were taught and sent to Africa as missionaries, so that
they could pray there with their brothers and sisters to
the Lord of all mankind. Years later we were forced to
put up with the Negro dwarf Rustimo as a playmate
for her youngest daughter. She had him baptized, giving
him the name of the crown prince, who even became
his godfather! A terrible creature, somewhere between
human and animal; moreover he chased the girls, until
he was drafted as a gardener. In Paris she dragged us
into a park where one could ride elephants, camels and
ostriches. She herself did not dare mount one of these
animals because of the scandal it might cause, but the
ladies and gentlemen of her entourage had to ride the
exotic creatures, which she found highly amusing. In her
apartments in the Hofburg monkeys would swing from
the gymnastic rings and curtains, parrots squawked and
dogs went chasing through the rooms. The monkeys were
the worst, screeching and, like cancan dancers, showing
off their polished backsides and brazen front parts so
provocatively that one no longer knew where to look.

*

When the taxi driver saw me he knew. Don't tell me,
you're going to the ball. You're already the third Sissi in
my cab this evening. After ten minutes we stopped outside a palais. Stuck to a poster stand was a likeness of
the empress, her hair glittering with diamond stars. A

lilac-coloured ribbon ran diagonally across the poster, announcing the theme of the ball: *Sissi for a Night*. In the picture Sissi had rather chubby cheeks and an obscenely fleshy neck. Ida paid with two notes and a coin, and waited for the exact change. She opened the car door for Frau Hohenembs and helped her out, while in my voluminous dress I hauled myself out of the taxi on my own. The tulle sash caught on the bodywork and I almost fell flat on my face. For goodness' sake, be careful, Frau Hohenembs cried. You'll ruin my dress. Heavens, you're so clumsy! By the way, do you think my neck is too fat? Jutting out her chin, she felt with both hands her skinny, wrinkled neck. I assured her that her neck was long and slim. The taxi drove off and we walked up the gravel drive to the illuminated palais, where countless women, some in ludicrous ball gowns, were already mingling. One girl with loose blonde hair was wearing a white, Empire-style dress that certainly wouldn't have been in fashion during Sissi's time – the soft, slack but also figure-hugging material would have been scandalous anywhere apart from in the theatre – while undressed hair would have been impossible, and on her head sat a diadem that bore greater resemblance to a monstrance than a crown. All of a sudden I felt silly in my dress and plaits. I found it childish to be without make-up and I hoped I wouldn't meet anyone I knew, even though an hour ago I'd still been full of excitement about the evening. Ida took the tickets from her handbag and we were each given a box with four Mozart balls as an offering. Ida unwrapped her chocolates and put them in her mouth. She chewed and swallowed them as if she were tucking into a slice of bread and butter. Why bother carrying them around? she replied to the look from Frau Hohenembs, who slipped her own box into the folds of her dress. I was undecided and hungry – in the last few days I'd eaten only vegetable broth and beef soup. Eating nothing at home isn't difficult. You know what you've let yourself in for, you've taken the appropriate precautions. But as soon as you find yourself somewhere else, outside or in the company of lots of other people, the feeling of hunger gnaws away at you like a persistent rodent. On the other hand, I didn't want to spoil my waist by eating sweet things now. Noticing my conflict, Frau Hohenembs took the decision for me by snatching the box out of my hand and giving it to Ida for safe keeping. Ida put it in her bag, which she clasped shut. I was sure she'd secretly eat the chocolates herself at the first opportunity, probably in the loo. While you're wearing this dress you're not going to eat a thing, do you understand? And certainly not chocolate. What on earth were you thinking? Frau Hohenembs threatened me with her index finger. But she was in a good mood and already striding through the crowd of people to the curved steps leading up to the entrance, Ida and I gliding in her wake. A swarm of Sissi imitations with their male companions, some in tails or dinner jackets, some in a sort of fantasy uniform and with stick-on Franz Joseph mutton chops, were clogging up the entrance to the ballroom, where a dancing master was just announcing a quadrille. We can't go in there, Frau Hohenembs groaned. I feel unwell with all these people around. We went down the steps on the other side and she directed us into the garden, which was decorated with colourful Chinese lanterns and garlands. There were fewer people here. Waiters swaggered across the lawn; we took a glass of Sekt and Frau Hohenembs toasted me. To you, the future Miss Sissi! Even Ida clinked glasses with me. Here's to you winning all those pralines! she cried, before downing her glass in one. It dawned on me that my life in the household of these two could become more difficult if I didn't win the pralines. I looked around; the other costumes were trashy and cheap, as Frau Hohenembs had predicted. Only a few were original or authentic. I could be content with my clothes; my hair was the only worry. It was too conservative and didn't match the historical prototype. We were approached by an elderly grey-haired man in tails, who tugged Frau Hohenembs's arm towards him to plant a kiss on her fingers. It didn't seem to bother him that in a hand-kiss the lips and fingers don't actually touch. Rather than letting go of her arm, he swung it back and forth in a fit of what seemed like childish pleasure. He bowed slightly to Ida and myself. Whom do we have here, dear Countess? he asked, squinting at me. This is a brand-new face. That's my niece, Baron Kalmar. She's going to take part in the Miss Sissi competition. With some effort Frau Hohenembs extracted her arm. Excuse me, Kalmar murmured. You understand. It's all right, Baron, it's all right, don't worry about it. We've known each other so long now... I'd never heard Frau Hohenembs talk to anybody with such affection. Only now did I notice that the baron suffered from a tic. He kept shifting from one foot to the other and his upper body moved from side to side. He tried to hide both his arms behind his back, but they shot out to the front, grabbing at invisible things in the air. *Formidable!* he cried. She's certainly got my vote. He waved to a waiter. I was so weak with hunger that I could barely stand on my own two legs. The Sekt was already going to my head and, like Ida, I knocked back the second glass, which Baron Kalmar offered me, just to get some calories. The baron spilled his drink on his tailcoat. We'll have that cleared up in a jiffy, Frau Hohenembs said, rubbing him with a cloth handkerchief, as the two of them giggled like adolescents. Ida opened her bag and took out a Mozart ball. I implored her to give me one or I'd die of hunger, so she unwrapped a chocolate for me and put it in my mouth. This came as such a surprise that I couldn't feel any disgust – the truth is, I hate being fed; it's an invasion of my privacy. I chewed and swallowed quickly so Frau Hohenembs wouldn't notice anything, but she was still busy with the baron, who was chuckling with joy. Ida gave me a second chocolate, which I practically swallowed whole, then she ate the final one herself. Would you please do me the honour of a dance? the baron begged Frau Hohenembs. But you know I don't dance, she replied.

He sighed. As inflexible as ever. Let's have another drink. He motioned again to a waiter; we drank our third glass and this time he managed not to spill a drop. Frau Hohenembs took a sip and tipped the rest into a plant pot. The baron bobbed up and down, threw his glass away for want of anywhere to put it down, licked his lips, squinted at me, then at Ida, as if unable to decide, and finally ventured an invitation. Frau Ida, would you? I was relieved that he hadn't asked me. Ida looked at the ground and whispered, But Herr Baron! Surely you will allow me, Countess, to abduct your Ida. Come, Frau Ida! Frau Hohenembs nodded; the baron grabbed Ida's arm and pulled her away. You smell delightfully of chocolate, we could hear him murmur before they dived into the sea of people. I took another glass of Sekt from a waiter's tray, to rinse out my mouth so Frau Hohenembs wouldn't smell the chocolate on my breath. Watch your drinking, she said. You look inebriated to me. I don't want you tumbling off the stage at midnight. I need the loo, I said, feeling disinhibited by the alcohol. Will you be all right on your own? Make sure you have a clear head, she called out as I left. And look after the dress! Don't you dare have anything to eat! I pushed past pseudo-Sissis and copycat Franz Josephs, and took a deep breath when I was out of Frau Hohenembs's sight. I wanted to go somewhere where I could relax, close my eyes and put my feet up, because the shoes were pinching. But the few seats were all occupied. As I passed the ballroom, I peered in, but I couldn't see Ida or the baron. Those inside were still dancing a quadrille; the two rows of men and women swayed towards each other, then joined up like the two sides of a zip. At the buffet people were piling rolls, lavish salads and breaded meat onto their plates. I didn't dare go any further into the room. They were wild animals scrambling for prey, and even if I had been certain that I could eat without making a mess, I was worried that one of the animals might tip a plate of egg salad down my dress. I was also thinking of my waist. At that very moment it was ideal; the dress was pleasantly slack and I didn't feel squeezed into it. Only the sleeves were tight. I couldn't puke in this dress and with these plaits. I could get a roll or two and eat them outside, to stave off the worst of the hunger, I thought. That way I'd be safe from the animals and I'd maintain my waist. But I knew myself. When I start, there's no stopping. Frau Hohenembs would kill me if she noticed a mark on the dress, I thought. And yet I was highly skilled at vomiting. In the past I'd thrown up while wearing all sorts of clothes and only seldom got dirty. But it was too risky. It didn't just depend on me, but on the loo; in some the water came too fast out of the cistern, in others the flow was gentler. I stood there indecisively, staring at the buffet. All of the sensible reasons I advanced against eating crumbled at the sight of this mountain of food, which the catering team kept piling up anew. What are you doing? I heard Ida whisper. Have you gone mad? You mustn't eat anything. Ida and the baron were standing arm in arm beside me, breathing heavily. Ida had red blotches all over her face and the baron looked like a tomcat who had just lapped up an entire bowl of cream. They were standing so close to one another, as if they were a pair of lovebirds, and the baron was bobbing from side to side and kept snuggling up to Ida. Please, get away from the buffet, Ida begged me. If the dress gets at all dirty then we're both in for it. This was the first time she'd ever lumped the two of us together. I attributed this to the fact that she'd been momentarily softened, no doubt by the baron's seed. I turned around and left the dining room. See you later, the baron called out after me. You can count on my vote! I stood in the queue for the loos and waited, letting through a few fake Sissis who were fidgeting and claiming they couldn't last a second longer. I was in no hurry myself, although the thought of Frau Hohenembs on her own in the garden made me uncomfortable. Ida and I delayed our return outside, although Ida had more fun than I did: sex and good food. I wandered around aimlessly, devoured by the thought of the buffet. And I was light years away from sex. I suspected that by now a storm was brewing inside Frau Hohenembs that would come thundering down on the two of us later. Maybe even on the baron; after all, he'd *abducted* Ida. The cubicles were spacious; I vomited. Then I returned to Frau Hohenembs. As I'd suspected, she was in a bad mood. Where on earth have you been? You need to put your name down for the competition. Ida hadn't reappeared yet. We can't wait for Ida; God only knows where she's got to. We have to put your name down now, she reiterated, pulling me by the arm all the way across the garden, the tight seam of the sleeve chafing my skin. In the furthest corner was a table where a man and woman were sitting, a list in front of them. Frau Hohenembs said my name and I was given a piece of cardboard with the number 169 on it, which I had to hold above my head when we paraded down the catwalk at midnight. My hopes vanished. There were bound to be more than 200 Sissis. The man from the voting committee put a sign on the table: *Entries close 23.50.* Frau Hohenembs checked her pocket watch. It's ten thirty now. And you're going to run rings around these cheap Sissis. I'm counting on you. Think of the pralines! We went back and saw in the distance Ida and the baron. He was clasping her arm and using the crowd to press up against Ida's body, which she happily complied with. You left me alone for a long time, Baron, Frau Hohenembs said with reproach in her voice. She didn't even glance at Ida. But the most gracious lady didn't wish to dance… the baron replied suggestively. Somehow I got the impression that he and Ida had had sex again in the meantime. They radiated such sated contentment, a blissfully distorted smile, which they neither could nor wanted to hide. I'm afraid I have to leave you, the baron said. I'm on the jury and we have a final meeting before the vote. You can be sure, he said, turning to me with a faintly jittery nod, that I shall do everything I can to ensure that you receive not only my vote. He kissed Frau Hohenembs's hand first, then Ida's, holding on to it for far too long and swinging it back and forth uncontrollably. Seemingly wanting to kiss the hand again, he changed his mind and flung it away violently. Ida cried out in horror. Pull yourself together! Frau Hohenembs barked. You're making yourself look ridiculous! Ida was beside herself, breathing heavily, and the blissful smile had now sunk into the downturned corners of her mouth; she was already suffering from her lover's absence.

*

My kedvesem would never have allowed me to marry. I was to belong to her alone. She was so terrified of being abandoned and would never have forgiven me. Not that I never had the opportunity: a marvellous, rich Russian count from St Petersburg courted me for months. I almost broke down and gave in. I loved the idea of living in my own castle as a Russian countess. There were also gentlemen from the royal household who wished to marry me, meaning I would not have had to leave the Hofburg palace. But I always bore in mind that a marriage would have banished me from her immediate proximity. She did not tolerate any married women as her friends. The only one who had been allowed to wed was the former theatrical hairdresser, Frau Feifalik. She could take all the liberties she liked; nothing was too much; even the emperor moaned about her. But of course she was the only one who was utterly indispensable! I had no desire to hurt my szeretett. Moreover, what could a man have offered me – even a terribly rich one – in comparison to her, my divine treasure who gave me everything?

*

An improvised stage made of wooden boards had been set up in the ballroom. Frau Hohenembs and Ida sat at a small table that the baron had reserved for them, and I went with my cardboard number through a side door into a neighbouring room, where more than 200 Sissis between the ages of fifteen and fifty were already waiting, all eager to step onto a catwalk at least once in their lives. We were called by number, our full names read out, and we had to walk one by one across the stage briskly, like models, with the cardboard number held above our heads, as a middle-aged woman with a blonde bun told us. With a few strides she showed us how she imagined models walk down the catwalk – an extremely aggressive and jaggedly nervous thrusting of the hips from side to side – and a few Sissis immediately started practising. The original Sissi was well known for her natural yet delicate gait, as if she were floating – precisely the opposite of what models do on the catwalk. Around half of the Sissis were, like me, wearing white dresses peppered with stars, although most of them were cheaply done; some even had large empty patches where the stars had already fallen off. There were stars in their hairdos too, and I also saw a few arrows of rhinestones or artificial flowers. The Sissi who stood out most was the blonde with the monstrance-like diadem; I thought she had the best chance, even though with her Empire-style dress she looked more like a woman from ancient Rome. But she had an easy-going air and beneath the pleated material there was an interesting figure. She was the only blonde, which I thought was original. I mingled with the 100 Sissis who were dressed like me. I imagined that from the auditorium it would be impossible to tell that my dress was more expensive and authentic than their cheap copies, more voluminous in the skirt part and more carefully worked. The only ace I had up my sleeve was the baron, but who could guarantee that, after espying some buxom wannabe Sissi, he wouldn't forget me altogether or be looking somewhere else as I came past? I was so far back in the queue that the jury must be asleep by my turn, dreaming of erotic adventures with hundreds of naked Sissis. The baron, at any rate, was only dreaming of Ida. Watch out, girls, here we go! the woman with the bun called out. Line up by number. The first ones at the front, the rest at the back! Those with low numbers thronged towards the door. No one would yield an inch. Number 3 was particularly pushy; she kept knocking into the women around her with her elbows and stood on lots of toes. There was a jumble of chatting, whispering and giggling. It reeked of pungent hairsprays, sweet lipsticks and sweat. In the ballroom a man was

speaking – we couldn't make out what he was saying
– then came a round of muted applause, and he said
something else that made the audience laugh and applaud
more loudly. Now the numbers were called at relatively
quick speed, and the girls stumbled towards the stage,
where a young man dragged them to the steps leading
up to the catwalk, which they staggered across before
being met by another man on the other side, who helped
them down the steps and directed them into another
room. You've got to hold up the numbers, the woman
with the bun hissed. Otherwise the jury won't know
who you are. This meant the first twenty had already
ruined their chances. The next twenty held their numbers
up high, which badly affected the way they walked; they
tripped, went too slowly or quickly, some ran, others
stopped and were barged into by the ones behind, who
shoved them along. Nobody had yet tried the classic
model walk. It was quiet offstage now. The Sissi hens
had shut up, each one concentrating hard to make sure
they didn't miss their name and number being called
out. Fifty had already gone. When I heard the number
169 I froze. The woman with the bun pushed me out,
the young man helped me onto the steps, whispering,
Number up! and all of a sudden I was on the wooden
planks in the blinding spotlights. The hall was a black
abyss; I felt giddy as I peered into this darkness, from
which I could hear an uncanny murmur. The abyss was
just waiting for something to happen so it could scream
and revel in a misfortune. Behind me, 170 and 171 were

pushing forward; 168 had already stepped off, but still I went slowly along the catwalk, carefully putting one foot in front of the other, as if walking across gravel, so as not to trip, and dutifully holding my number aloft, hoping that no one would recognize me. The boards were fairly uneven; I had to take care, especially in Frau Hohenembs's shoes, which I wasn't used to and which, or so it seemed to me at least, were getting tighter with every step. I was pleased to make it to the other side without mishap and to be able to disappear among all those Sissis I didn't know. Here were chaos and tears. The first twenty Sissis knew they had muffed their chance – no number, no rating – their faces were red and swollen from crying, and smeared with make-up. The floor was littered with stars that had fallen off, ribbons and scraps of material hung over the cheap imitation Biedermeier chairs, and the girls were stuffing their faces with the greasy egg mayonnaise and salmon rolls that were being handed around. Others who fancied their chances were eating and drinking as much as they could so that they'd weigh a few hundred grams or even a kilo more on the scales and thus win more pralines. I was so starving that I grabbed at the rolls with both hands and tucked in as if I were alone in my bedroom. No one was watching me, fortunately; all the Sissis were too preoccupied with themselves. I'd just polished off my tenth roll, the dress was feeling uncomfortably tighter at the waist, when a fanfare came from the hall and the man who'd spoken at the beginning – this time he had a microphone – announced that the jury would now consult to choose fifteen Sissis for the final, from which one would be elected jointly by the jury and the audience as Miss Sissi 2007. This was new; we'd thought that the jury would elect the eventual Sissi winner. It meant that the trembling was not yet over; the fifteen finalists would have to get up on the catwalk again, the woman with the bun explained. The mouths smeared with lipstick and mayonnaise gaped in horror. Half of the Sissis were deranged and a hectic wiping with tissues and napkins began, an adjusting of hairdos, some even gathered up stars from the floor to tack them onto their dresses and heads. The rolls were repeating on me; thank goodness there was a loo here. The Sissis were shoving themselves in front of the mirrors. I locked myself in a cubicle, gathered up the skirt part of the dress as best I could, pushing it up so it didn't touch the floor and holding it with one hand, clasping my plaits to the back of my head with the other, and carefully began retching up the salmon and mayonnaise mush. A repulsive fishy smell spread around me. I let go of the plaits and flushed while I was still puking. The plaits sprang forward and the brush-like ends were splashed with water. From the next-door cubicle I heard spitting, retching and a hysterical coughing. It didn't sound like deliberate vomiting, but who could tell? I checked the dress for marks; I appeared to have been lucky. I felt better; it was loose around my waist again and my head was clearer. I rinsed out my mouth. It was quiet in the hall, a fanfare sounded again and the host read out fifteen names and numbers. I was the last. I gave a start, although I also found it perfectly understandable. The blonde with the monstrance was also among the finalists. We were to come out slowly in single file and turn from one side to the other on the stage. Where's your number? the woman with the bun hissed. She was right; my hands were empty, that's why I'd felt so unencumbered. I've left it in the loo, I told her. Go and get it, quick! I ran back and found the piece of cardboard on the floor in the cubicle. It was filthy, with dark shoe marks, because someone had trampled on it – me probably, while I was throwing up – but you could still see the number. We proceeded in single file, the band played a march, and then we stood on the catwalk, holding aloft our numbers. Unsure of how to stand, we turned now to the left, now to the right, no doubt looking like embarrassed school-girls at our leavers' ball. The audience started shouting out numbers until the host intervened and explained the procedure. He would call each number again and the audience had to clap. The intensity of the applause would be measured by a machine and then the jury would pick and crown their Miss Sissi from the three with the most applause. After a fanfare he began calling out the finalists one by one; they took a step forward and curtsied. After the first had done it the rest copied. When it was my turn I gave a little curtsy too – I didn't know what else to do – and held my soiled cardboard number above my head. Then they compared the levels of applause and the final three were: me, the blonde and a fifty-year-old Sissi in riding gear and a top hat. The rest stepped down from the stage, accompanied by a melancholy march. The host pointed to us with his outstretched arm. Ladies and gentlemen, the final three! he exclaimed, like a barker at a fair. A fanfare, then applause surged from the dark abyss. The blonde and I smiled at each other, while the equestrian Sissi remained serious. She was fairly old; you could see that she envied our youth, which made her a little older still, but her costume with the top hat looked good on her, and I expect we all appeared the same age to the audience. The host bent over the jury's table and asked whether they had reached a decision. A spotlight was aimed at the members of the jury; I saw the baron nod and drum on the table with his fingers. We have a unanimous decision, he said. A fanfare, silence, the baron couldn't restrain himself any longer. It's number 169! he cried, leaping up and starting to clap. The audience joined in, as did the host, whose announcement, Ladies and gentlemen, I give you Miss Sissi 2007, was totally lost amidst the noise. At that moment a huge set of scales was pushed onto the stage, together with a wheelbarrow containing dozens of boxes of pralines. It was uplifting, unfortunately. The equestrian Sissi offered me her hand and her congratulations – she looked relieved – while the blonde Sissi went so far as to embrace me, causing her monstrance to slip. She took the diadem off her head and waved to the audience with it. The host gave both of them a box of chocolates and led them off the stage. Then he took me by the arm to the scales. Some steps were rolled on, he helped me onto one side of the scales by holding my arm, then began to fill the other side with pralines. An assistant counted. The host tossed in box after box while reeling off his jokes. I was glad to be able to sit finally – the scales were comfortable, and without thinking about it I took off my shoes and rubbed my feet. My side of the scales slowly started to rise, and when he reached the hundred and second packet, the two sides were balanced at the same height. There were fifty-one kilos of me and fifty-one kilos of pralines. I was horrified, but then it occurred to me that the dress must weigh at least three kilos, and there were the shoes, so I was under fifty kilos. Another fanfare. The assistant heaved me out of the scales and, while the host led me off, the assistant packed the boxes of pralines into two sacks and carried them behind me after I'd staggered off the stage – the young men who'd helped us get up and down earlier on were nowhere to be seen. Ida waved from a table at which Frau Hohenembs and the baron were also sitting, and I fought my way through the clapping and grinning crowd, followed by the assistant with the sacks. The baron gave him a glass of champagne. Frau Hohenembs nodded and said, Well done, I'm pleased with you. Ida gazed at the sacks; the assistant downed a second glass and left. I remembered the shoes; I hadn't realized I'd walked off the stage in stockings. I ran after the assistant and asked him to bring me the shoes I'd left on the scales. Stop! Where are you going? I heard Frau Hohenembs call out. I explained that I'd taken off the shoes on the scales and left them there. How could you? Frau Hohenembs snapped. Whatever made you take off *my* shoes? Now, now, the baron said, it's no great calamity, I'm sure those little shoes will turn up again. But they didn't. The assistant came back without them, assuring us he'd looked everywhere. Frau Hohenembs punished me in the taxi home with her silence.

*

At Carnival time she once went dressed as a yellow domino to the masquerade ball in Vienna – incognito, of course – and I had to accompany her. I found a young man for her, with whom she spoke and joked; indeed, my normally aloof mistress even dared to flirt. Their conversation lasted for hours. The young man soon guessed who he had before him, but he did not dare to ask her directly. In the end I had to insist that we leave the ball and take our carriage home – who knows what might have happened otherwise? As we left he tried to remove her mask and give her a kiss, which fortunately I was able to prevent. He followed us for a while and she instructed the carriage driver to take a different route; only after an hour was he allowed to go the right way. She remained preoccupied by this adventure for a long while; she even wrote the unlucky fellow a few letters, to which he responded in rather bold language. Later, in spite of her express wishes, he did not want to return the letters.

*

I had to stand still in the drawing room while Frau Hohenembs walked around me, inspecting the dress. The dog followed her in a circle. She opened up the folds in the material, felt the stars and lifted up the skirt part. Luckily she didn't find any stains or marks. Then Ida had to undress me. I stood before Frau Hohenembs in my knickers and stockings, and she examined me from head to toe. The dog pressed his damp, hairy muzzle between my legs. It was only with difficulty that I was able to keep his enormous head at a distance. Frau Hohenembs did nothing. I think we'll leave the weigh-in today; we've already had that, haven't we? You can throw the stockings away; I don't imagine they can be worn again. The stockings were hers too; only the knickers were mine. I went to my room, slamming the door in the dog's face, and lay down on the bed. A few minutes later he was scratching at the door. I took off the stockings, which were black and torn at the toes and calves. I scrunched them up and tossed them into a corner. I was hungry, but decided not to eat anything. You lose weight most quickly by refraining from eating for a good while after being sick, especially before going to bed. I stroked my belly, which was reassuringly flat.

My hipbones were sticking out, just as they ought to, and I felt an inner peace. Everything was all right if I was thin. I caressed my stomach again, stroking around the belly button, which was no more than a narrow slit, and took off my knickers. I smoothed down my pubic hair, pulled it apart, stroked it flat, wrapped it around my finger, making little ringlets. I pondered shaving it all off. But for whom? It was too late for Charlotte. I felt my body a while longer until I fell asleep. When I came into the kitchen the following morning Ida was already sitting at the table in her housecoat, with a cup of coffee and a glass of water that was bubbling and fizzing – Alka-Seltzer or Aspirin C. She'd piled up the boxes of pralines beside her. It smelled of violets and chocolate and faintly of paper, too. She looked at me. Isn't that a magnificent sight? Have you already opened a box? I asked. I'd love to try one. She took a box and gave it to me. This is for you; we can only open the rest with *her* express permission. I poured myself a glass of water and sat at the table with Ida to gaze at the mountain of boxes. It instilled fear in me – I didn't want to live in the same household as fifty kilograms of chocolate. Especially not if they were lying around in the kitchen like this. What's going to happen to these now? The pralines will be locked in a cupboard; she'll count them every day, Ida replied. There are now 100 boxes. I've got one too, she added. As she didn't offer me anything from her box, I assumed that she'd already eaten her share. I've got to make breakfast now, she said as moodily as ever, standing up. I went to my room with the box of pralines and put them with the rest of my supplies. As a child, before going to sleep I'd often imagine living life as a hermit. I'd dwell alone in the forest, in a small hut in a glade, with a huge supply of food, like a mountain of nuts that would slowly get smaller. Every day I'd crack and eat a precise amount. The important thing about my fantasy was my stock of supplies and the fact that I'd foraged, cooked or hunted everything myself. I was always alone, too. Nobody visited me in the forest, I wasn't waiting for anyone. There was no conceivable end to my retreat. After a year was over I had to replenish my supplies. When I was older I got hold of a book in the city library describing how a forty-year-old woman found herself all alone in a hunting lodge, surrounded, at a distance of several kilometres, by an impenetrable, transparent, smooth wall – or was it a dome? At any rate, she had to spend the rest of her life in this hunting lodge. All she possessed was a dog, a cow and a cat; she lived according to the seasons, leading the cow to pasture, gathering berries, even planting potatoes, chopping, drying and stacking wood. The very first day she realized she would never escape this confinement she pushed her bed into the kitchen and sealed off all the other rooms. The kitchen was the centre of her life. As I read the book I recalled my childhood pre-sleep fantasies and felt a comforting connection with the author. She had expressed my feelings precisely. The protagonist, however, shared her existence with animals who guaranteed her survival. I'd never allowed myself such a luxury. It was irresistible to be so utterly dependent on yourself, to undertake physical work to guarantee your day-to-day survival, to get along with simple things. The idea of stockpiling something to be able to live off it later I found appealing. To have no past and no future, living in a permanently constant present, thinking only of the future in terms of wondering how and when you'd begin to stock up your supplies, and scouring the past for possible errors so as to avoid making them in the future. I didn't envisage what would later happen in real life – me devouring all the supplies in one go. I felt uneasy about the stock of pralines in the kitchen. My supplies had to remain reasonable. There was silence at breakfast. Frau Hohenembs drank her meat juice, Ida ate pastries, I was undecided. Should I stick to my diet like before the ball? I drank coffee with lots of milk and cream and decided that I'd stick to liquids for today. Frau Hohenembs instructed Ida to bake a Gugelhupf because the baron was coming to tea that afternoon. She should make something light for lunch, maybe a soup. Ida's face lit up and she cleared the table. It's time for you to give me my injection now, Frau Hohenembs said to me. I administered the cocaine to her, which by now I could do without any difficulty. No more was said about the ball; I'd fulfilled my task, but lost the shoes, there was no more to say about it. Then the Greek teacher came and I withdrew to my room as usual. When I heard the door shut later I knew the lesson was over and lunch would be on the table in half an hour.

*

On Corfu she was always very reclusive; I hardly saw my édes lelkem apart from when she was having her hair dressed, during which time she would issue her instructions. I felt lonely, abandoned; I longed for Gödöllő, where she was never so distant from me. Hungary always brought us closer together. Here in Greece I was like a stranger to her. The Achilleion, as she called her house, had been built as a mixture of antique-like elements and modern technology. The entire house was electrified and a small powerhouse was set up to provide the electricity. Electric flames shone from the hands of stucco Cupids in the form of fruits or bubbles. There were many rooms whose walls and ceilings were decorated with replicas of Pompeiian frescoes. The furniture and fittings were inlaid with mosaics. Although they were magnificently padded, the chairs were uncomfortable to sit on, because 2,000 years ago people had different habits, she told me. I never really understood this; to me sitting seems such a timeless activity that there cannot be so many options. For her that was irrelevant; she did not like sitting down. All that counted was the aesthetic impression.

*

The baron stuck a finger through the bars of the parrot cage. Careful, Frau Hohenembs called out. Their beaks are sharp! The birds pecked at his finger, but the baron pulled it out in time. They squawked, cackled and ruffled their feathers. The baron turned away and admired the Gugelhupf that Ida was just carrying in. Frau Ida, did you make that yourself? It looks delicious! Ida turned red. She had already taken off her housecoat before the baron arrived, which meant that her décolletage was flaunting a circle of icing sugar, almost like a piece of jewellery. Frau Hohenembs had failed to remark on it. Ida had never taken her coat off for the Greek teacher, nor had she ever paraded her décolletage; her dresses were always buttoned up to the neck. She looked really good. There was just one thing that marred her appearance: the bitten fingernails with traces of dried blood. Licking his lips, the baron sat down at Frau Hohenembs's table. Only then did Ida and I sit too. Frau Hohenembs poured the tea and handed round the cake that Ida had already sliced. The baron rocked in his chair, ate several pieces of cake and praised Ida's baking skills. He looked longingly at her patch of icing sugar, which stood out against her reddened skin. Ida was so excited that she couldn't eat a thing and had only two cups of tea, which she drank in tiny sips rather than gulping as usual. Her hands were trembling and the cup clattered against the saucer when she put it down. Frau Hohenembs gnawed away at her piece of cake, while I helped myself to a second slice. I hadn't eaten much yet – a bowl of potato

soup at lunch – so I could allow myself this. The dog
lay at Frau Hohenembs's feet, occasionally lifting his
head to growl at the baron. It was obvious that Frau
Hohenembs and I were superfluous in this room – the
parrots were no longer bothering anyone – but how were
they going to get rid of us? The baron and Frau
Hohenembs engaged in meaningless conversation; Frau
Hohenembs appeared to find the baron's lack of attention amusing. Ida became increasingly nervous and
finally she took a piece of cake after all. Now there was
icing sugar at the corners of her mouth too and the
baron leaped up, as if about to rush and lick it off, but
then he fell back down into his chair with a sigh. I'm
sorry, he said to Frau Hohenembs. My illness, you know.
I do know. Calm yourself, my dear Baron, you don't
have to apologize. Ida stood up to brew a new pot of
tea, as she said. This was the code word. Now the baron
just needed to find an excuse to go into the kitchen too.
I'll help you, Frau Ida, he called out, and followed her.
Frau Hohenembs giggled behind her hand. Go into the
kitchen, she said a few minutes later, having composed
herself. Cast an eye over them! Reluctantly, I stood up.
What these turtle doves got up to was no business of
mine. I moved slowly towards the kitchen and peered
through the crack in the door. It was too late. Ida lay
on her stomach across the kitchen table, her huge snow-
white bottom shining brightly out of the black material
pushed up her back. He kneaded it like dough, shook
icing sugar onto it, took a lick, then a bite, and poked

around the bum crack with his thumb. Finally he pulled down his trousers, spread Ida's bum cheeks, penetrated her, grabbed onto her waist and fucked her with rapid movements. They made no noise save for a suppressed moan; I could just hear the table wobbling. I watched the two bodies in fascination. Two walruses. A shudder went through the baron's body and he stopped before marshalling all his strength for one last thrust. Ida cried out softly. Stephan, she sighed. He lay on top of her, grunting. I withdrew. What's going on in there? asked Frau Hohenembs, who was coming towards me in the hallway, the dog behind. She pushed me to one side; I couldn't stop her from barging into the kitchen. The baron was still inside Ida, who was whimpering quietly. Well, I never, Frau Hohenembs exclaimed. Baron, go downstairs at once, how could you! The baron rolled off Ida, but had the presence of mind to pull down Ida's dress and so cover her bottom. He pulled up his trousers. Please excuse me, Countess, Frau Ida and I, we're terribly fond of each other. He was tottering. Ida hid behind the baron's back. My most revered Countess von Hohenembs he said, taking a deep breath and standing up straight, I should like to ask for the hand of your Frau Ida in marriage. My intentions are wholly honourable. I should like to marry and look after her; you know I have sufficient financial means at my disposal. I will protect her like the apple of my eye, of that you can be absolutely certain. For a few seconds Frau Hohenembs was speechless. You must be out of your mind, dear

Baron; there can be absolutely no talk of marriage, heaven forbid! One doesn't get married at Ida's age, it's disgusting! She practically spat out these last words and Ida started crying. I must ask you to leave my apartment, Baron! The baron looked undecided as to whether he should obey the command or take Ida with him. Turning around, he whispered something into Ida's ear, making her sob even more. I'm going! he said theatrically. But I'll be back, Countess! He kissed the forehead of the weeping Ida and staggered out of the kitchen. His arms flapped all over the place uncontrollably; by accident the back of his hand hit the dog's head. The dog howled and fled under the table Ida was sitting on. The door closed; it sounded exactly as if the Greek teacher had just left the apartment. Get down from that table, Ida, and stop your sobbing. And as for you, clear up the drawing room, she snapped at me. She pulled the dog out from under the table by his collar and took him into her bedroom. I brought the crockery and the rest of the cake into the kitchen. Ida hadn't budged; she was still sitting at the table, whining away to herself. I put the dirty crockery in the dishwasher and wrapped the cake in cellophane. I picked up Ida's scrunched-up panty girdle from the floor and draped it over a chair, then poured a glass of water and handed it to her. Thanks, she muttered. She gulped it down in one go and gave me the glass back. Do you really want to marry the baron? I asked. She nodded. Why don't you just go away with him, then? I can't. She'd report me to the police straight away. But she's the mastermind behind it all! I cried. That's true, but she's got friends everywhere; she could wriggle her way out of anything. When I was young I let myself become involved in something dreadful for her, a misdemeanour for which there is no statute of limitations. It's hopeless, she sighed. And then there's the baron. You see, the baron talks a good game. But he's married, so he'd have to get a divorce first, and his wife would never allow that. His fortune comes from her; if they got divorced he'd lose everything. He can't look after me like he says; that just came out in the heat of the moment. And *she* knows it. She'll never give me Corfu and you'll never get Wachtel's apartment! Does it even exist? I asked. Even if Wachtel does die soon, she won't give you the flat; she'll put it off as she's done with me. Ida started weeping again, then Frau Hohenembs was right beside us. What are you two whispering about? Get on with your work, Ida. And you, go to your room. You've caused enough trouble today! It's all your fault, she said, pointing to the door with her arm outstretched. I had no idea why it should be all my fault, but Ida's destiny was my destiny, which suddenly flashed before my eyes menacingly. I saw myself, old and wrinkled, sitting by Frau Hohenembs's bed, condemned to care for her and Ida, and when the two of them were dead it would be too late for me, my life long since over. Even if he couldn't marry her, perhaps the baron would be able to help Ida escape, and me too. All he'd have to do would be to get us fake passports. He must be a

Hungarian, going by his name at least. The destiny of a fellow countrywoman must lie close to his heart. Ida and I could flee to Hungary. Surely there must be people in Budapest who needed someone to declutter their houses. Perhaps Hungary was too close. Perhaps Frau Hohenembs's contacts stretched as far as Budapest. I'd have to discuss it with Ida.

*

Hungary was her fairy-tale country. My szeretett angyalom never espoused a cause like she did the Hungarian one. The Dual Monarchy was her work. She was irresistibly attracted to the passion and informality of the Hungarians, in contrast to the ceremony-heavy Viennese court life with its impenetrable intrigues and sensibilities, where each archduke built up his own little court whose task was to oppose the others. She always hated that. In Hungary she could breathe, there she was venerated and admired, she was left in peace; in her beloved Gödöllő she could recover from the vulgarities of everyday life in Vienna. She could go riding whenever she wanted, without being gawped at or having to worry about public criticism.

*

Frau Hohenembs no longer let us out of her sight, we had to go for walks with her, she gave us errands we had to run separately from each other. I still didn't have my own set of keys. Even at night Frau Hohenembs would stay up, wander round the apartment, hang on the rings in the door frame, put on the *Sissi* videos or pseudo-documentaries about cosmetic surgery to make us believe that she'd be spending a quiet hour or two in the TV chair, but then she'd turn up unexpectedly in every room in the apartment. A confidential conversation with Ida was impossible. The parrots rasped ill-temperedly to themselves and pecked at the bars if you got close to their cage. They weren't parroting back what we said any more. Ida and I had to be present at the Greek lessons and repeat the Greek phrases without knowing what they meant. Ida couldn't start making lunch until after the lesson. A little education won't harm you; one's never too old to learn a new language, Frau Hohenembs said waspishly. Hungarian would be better, I thought, and refused to repeat Greek words any differently from a parrot. But I didn't learn Hungarian either; I didn't have any time. When I was in my room I stuffed myself with violet pralines and other food, and just as they were beginning to be digested I'd let them surge back into the jars in a gooey flood. Then I'd lie on my bed and stare at the ceiling. The mountain of boxes in the cupboard grew smaller; Ida, too, took out her daily ration and Frau Hohenembs hadn't said anything yet. The baron didn't come back to the apartment; Ida would meet up with him when she was out shopping or running errands for Frau Hohenembs. She returned from these errands with the same expression on her face that I'd seen at the ball. Frau Hohenembs complained that Ida took too long, she was never there when she was needed, she really shouldn't dawdle. She increasingly sent me out instead. Then the baron would approach, trembling and skipping from the other side of the road, and ask after Ida – wasn't she coming out today? The first time we met I asked him outright whether he could help us escape, get us passports, take us over the border and hide us in Budapest. Impossible, he said, he was under an obligation to Frau Hohenembs, he couldn't go behind her back, and, in any case, he had no idea how to get passports and he didn't have any connections in Hungary; he'd been separated from his home country for too long. His secret meetings with Ida were risky enough – if his wife found out, that was it. Looking at me, he said sadly, You're still young, you attach such importance to every word. A man will say anything to wriggle out of a difficult situation. By the next day he's totally forgotten what he said. It doesn't worry him any more. Ida knows this; she's a woman of experience. Think about it whenever a man makes you a promise. He walked away, swinging his arms. I did my shopping and went to sit on a park bench opposite my old flat. The windows had been cleaned recently and reflected the sunlight like mirrors. If only I could turn back time and stand at those windows again to look out at the park. I cursed the day Frau Hohenembs had spoken to me outside the patisserie. How often had I imagined someone sitting on this bench, watching my windows or me wandering about in the flat? It would never have occurred to me that I might be sitting here one day, wishing I could have my old life back. A cloud blocked out the sun for a few minutes and I could see that the blinds were down, but the slats were horizontal. A silhouette moved behind one of the windows and for a second I thought it was Charlotte. Then the sun came back out and I was looking at the reflecting panes of glass once more. Picking up the shopping bags, I returned to Frau Hohenembs's apartment. I rang and she opened the door at once, as if she'd been waiting there the whole time. What took you so long? she cried. I could have sent Ida instead. She dragged me in and shut the door. Come on, come on, Ida's waiting for those things to make lunch. We're already late again! And besides, if you think I haven't noticed that you and Ida are stealing pralines from the cupboard then you're very much mistaken. You'd better watch it! Without saying a word, I went into the kitchen and put the shopping on the table. What more can she do to me? I thought. I decided I'd escape alone. In any case, I couldn't rely on Ida; she'd long since resigned herself to her fate and was enjoying some late-found happiness with the baron, which she surely couldn't ever have anticipated. She didn't believe in Corfu any more. And there was no way she'd give up the baron. The baron himself was quite content with this little liaison that brightened up his days, and he certainly wouldn't gamble it on some questionable adventure that held nothing in prospect for him. I decided that, as soon as Frau Hohenembs sent me on another errand, I'd go to Vienna South station and jump on a train to Bratislava. Within an hour I'd be over the border in Slovakia with my own passport before Frau Hohenembs had noticed that I was missing. From Bratislava I could go on to Prague or Berlin. There must be desperate people in Berlin, too, who needed help decluttering. The key thing was that there mustn't be too much time between leaving the apartment and the train's departure. I didn't know how many trains a day went to Bratislava. Hopefully more than just one or two. I also needed cash. Which meant I'd have to save up my pocket money. My stomach tightened. Full of hatred, I looked at my tummy. It was almost flat. If I stood up straight it curved outwards very slightly. Only if I pulled it in was it concave. But I didn't want to pull it in any more. I no longer wanted to let my belly govern my life. I weighed forty-seven kilograms. That was a good weight; I could put on three kilos or lose a couple without a bad conscience – it didn't matter. At this weight I was in the safety zone. I checked my supplies. A wrapped-up marble cake, biscuits, banana chips. The provisions for my escape. I counted my money: ten euros. That would get me to Bratislava at most. My savings had long since gone. Unfortunately, I didn't know where Frau Hohenembs kept her money. The coins had been a stroke of luck. I could have taken a few items of jewellery – she often left stuff lying around in the drawing room – but where and how would I sell them? Ida managed the housekeeping money. She always took the notes from the pocket sewn onto her housecoat, as if she harboured an inexhaustible source of money. It was too risky to ask Ida for cash. Even though she'd been much more affable recently, I didn't trust her. She remained loyal to Frau Hohenembs and her affair with the baron was probably the most she dared undertake. Perhaps I could tap the baron for some money. If I threatened to spill the beans about his affair to his wife. But wouldn't he tell Ida straight away? I needed a plausible reason why he should keep it quiet from Ida. Perhaps by using the same threat: if he told Ida, I'd tell his wife. The ideal scenario would be to get the money on the day of my escape. In any case, he was always standing at the corner waiting for Ida, and he'd make a long face if I came out instead of her. Once I had to free him from a dog that had run around him several times with its lead. The strap had got hooked onto a piece of metal sticking out from a road sign and the baron ended up being tied to it. The owner only came strolling along a few minutes later. He didn't apologize and took the lead from me without saying anything. The baron was so ashamed that he didn't utter a word either. We could go to the bank together; it wouldn't have to be much, 3,000 euros, say. He couldn't refuse me that. I hoped that he had his own money; he had bragged about his finances when proposing marriage, but that could have all been a lie. Maybe his wife allowed him a small amount of pocket money,

just as with Frau Hohenembs and me. When she sent
me to the dressmaker's to fetch some sort of bodice, I
went into an internet café and printed out the timetable
from Vienna to Bratislava. To my surprise there was a
train every thirty minutes and the journey took just over
an hour. The last one was at 00.12, the first at 05.28. I
could get a train any time of day. I couldn't find out
about trains from Bratislava to Prague; the site kept
crashing. It didn't matter, as I suspected that Frau
Hohenembs didn't have contacts in Slovakia or the Czech
Republic any longer, and certainly not with the police.
She spoke Hungarian but no Czech or Slovak. I packed
my handbag – passport, toothbrush, three pairs of
knickers, address book, timetable and the wrapped-up
marble cake – so that I'd be ready any time Frau
Hohenembs sent me on an errand. When we ate together
Ida would pile up my plate with food that I barely
touched. I was too nervous. You've got to eat, she said
with concern in her voice, You're getting awfully thin.
Leave her alone, Frau Hohenembs said. Don't always
force people to eat. I mean, heaven forbid it wouldn't
do you any harm to eat less and get rid of some of that
fat. And when are you finally going to stop chewing
your nails? Ida said nothing, but still stuck to her eating
habits: lots and fast. Over the next few days I lurked
around Ida and kept asking her whether she needed
anything from the supermarket. I thought she must have
noticed, but she didn't seem to smell a rat. After all, she
took every opportunity to leave the apartment herself.

And then came the moment. Frau Hohenembs wanted me to take some shoes to the cobbler's. I took the box with the shoes and my handbag, and left the apartment. I wondered where I should throw away the shoes – right here or at the station – and opted for the station. The baron was not in his usual place. Blood rushed straight to my head. I waited at the corner for a while, shifting from one foot to the other, swinging the box of shoes to and fro as if imitating the baron's tic, and looked out for him – he'd probably just popped into a café. Then I remembered that Ida had gone shopping that morning; of course, he didn't need to wait for her any more. Which was one thing I hadn't accounted for in my plan – it could only work on a day when Ida hadn't been out before me. Downcast, I went to the Turkish cobbler's and handed over the shoes. He gave me an orange receipt. The shoes would be ready in a week. Two days later Frau Hohenembs sent both Ida and me shopping, something she hadn't done since the scandalous episode with the baron. I didn't even bother taking my handbag. The baron was already fidgeting on the other side of the street. We'd meet up again in an hour. She came back without the baron, but with her blissful smile. At home Frau Hohenembs started berating her: What do you think you're grinning at? Concentrate on the washing! I've got nothing left to wear. Ida opened the door to her bedroom; the dog was lying among all the unironed laundry. He'd messed everything up and the laundry was full of dog hairs. Ida shooed him away. The washing would have to be done again. I was convinced that Frau Hohenembs had deliberately let the dog into Ida's room. I went to the kitchen and put the shopping in the fridge. From the drawing room, Frau Hohenembs ordered me to make some tea and open a box of pralines. As I was bringing both into her, the box of pralines slipped from my hand and the confectionery fell on the table and floor, where it was immediately gobbled up by the dog. He moved his muzzle along the parquet like a Hoover. What is wrong with the two of you? Frau Hohenembs ranted. You're useless, both of you! And when are you finally going to wear a housecoat? I can't watch you any more. I fetched a glass bowl, gathered up the rest of the pralines and plonked them on the table. Never, I spat between my teeth. I'm never going to wear a housecoat. I retired to my room. Useless, useless, the parrots called out after me. It was the first thing they'd said since the ball. All I needed now was for Frau Hohenembs to start calling me by my first name. But I'd be long gone by them. The following morning Frau Hohenembs gave me 100 euros and the address of a shop that sold work clothes. She told me to go there and buy two or three housecoats. No more buts! My continual objections were ridiculous – as if wearing one was going to hurt! My housecoats didn't have to be white like Ida's; I could choose the colour and pattern I wanted. It was morning, Ida had not yet been out, I'd need longer than an hour for this errand, Frau Hohenembs wouldn't wonder where I was until after two or even three hours, I had 100 euros in addition to whatever I could blackmail the baron for and the banks were open. Taking the money and my handbag, I waved goodbye. Well, well, Frau Hohenembs said, no objections this time? You're right, I replied. It *is* childish of me. I'm sure a housecoat will be very practical.

*

Secret agents had a colossal job with her. My kedvesem used to go out for walks at the oddest hours; it was not uncommon to find her taking a stroll in the woods at three in the morning. The emperor had assigned them the task of being on their guard day and night, and not to let her out of their sight under any circumstances. But few people were as fit as she. She could hike for eight hours in the most difficult terrain, without displaying any tiredness. What is more, the secret agents were to stalk her unobtrusively, so she did not notice; they had to keep at least 200 metres away from her at all times. For she hated nothing more than being spied upon. The agents would hide behind trees and rocks, but that did not help. She always noticed when they were on her tail, and she almost always managed to shake off the portly officials. If necessary she would leap over a fence like a deer, or vanish onto secret, dark paths that only she knew.

*

Rather than waste any time on small talk, I offered a brief explanation before demanding money from the baron. Well I never, he said, but then agreed to the blackmail. In a brief spasm he shook himself like a wet dog. His branch was a couple of streets further down, he said. He could withdraw the 3,000 euros there. He gave it to me in the foyer in an envelope containing ten-euro and hundred-euro notes. Well, well, a young woman like you and then something like this. You're not living up to your title; our empress would be turning in her grave. To begin with, I didn't know what he was talking about, but then I remembered the Miss Sissi competition. What do you need the money for anyway? he asked. I didn't reply, but gave a terse Thanks. We went our separate ways; I don't know if he returned to his spot to wait for Ida. I ran for the bus that was going to the station. A train for Bratislava was leaving in twenty minutes. At the station I bought a single ticket, some mineral water, a newspaper, and got on the train. I was free! The train set off. I was alone in the compartment. An intricate nexus of railway tracks and graffiti-covered station buildings passed by, overgrown green areas with decommissioned carriages and crumbling factories or orange-brick warehouses. I was comforted by the clickety-clack of the train rolling across the sleepers. Maybe Charlotte could join me later. She'd always said she didn't want to remain in Vienna for ever. I opened my bag to check the contents. Passport, money, marble cake, knickers – everything was there. I leafed through the newspaper without being able to take anything in. It was almost exactly an hour since I'd left Frau Hohenembs's apartment. She wouldn't be missing me yet. By the time she started to become suspicious I'd be over the border and – if I was lucky – already on a train to Prague. At the border the train stopped and customs officers boarded with Bernese mountain dogs on short leashes. The dogs' black coats with the red-and-white badges gleamed in the sun. The compartment doors were opened and the customs officers politely asked to see passports. Three of them came in while a fourth stayed outside with a dog. One officer took my passport and gave it a lengthy examination, scrutinizing the photograph. You've got a different hairstyle, he said in a friendly tone. Yes, I said. So? We've got to take you with us, please get out! Because my hair's different? Which woman has the same hairstyle as on her passport photo? They didn't give me an answer, but kept hold of the passport, and I had to leave the train with them. I pressed my handbag to my body. They couldn't take my money, could they? Had the baron filed a complaint? They were not interested in my bag, but took me to the customs booth, where I had to wait. A Bernese mountain dog lay down on my feet and fell asleep. The train left. After half an hour of sitting uncomfortably and with hot feet because of the dog, two police officers came. A man and a woman – I recognized them immediately in spite of their uniform. It was the couple who'd taken over my flat. Now it dawned on me where I'd seen them even before then:

in the supermarket. The detective who'd found the tins of caviar in my bag and the woman who'd come to my assistance. They told me to accompany them. I looked at the customs officer sitting at the desk, typing something into his computer. He handed me over to his supposed colleagues and went back to his work without glancing up. He wasn't interested in what happened to me. I should have shouted, begged him not to leave me at the mercy of fake police officers, I should have been able to tell him the story about the supermarket, the flat and the intrigue involving the property-management company. He wouldn't have believed me, of course. The two agents must have counterfeit papers identifying themselves as police officers. Don't start getting any silly ideas! If you make things difficult we'll put you in handcuffs. They moved to either side of me, each of them taking an arm, and led me to their car. They sat me in the back, locked both doors from the outside and got in the front. A glass partition reinforced with metal rods separated the front and back seats. I put my forehead against the window. The wind turbines with their slim, white propellers waved from the distance, the flat fields looked like enormous green carpets covering the landscape, hiding who knew what beneath. The flat vineyards I could never get used to – for me, vineyards have to be hilly, even steep; a proper wine has to come from a slope – the crouched, whitewashed winemakers' houses, all this flew past a second time, now in the opposite direction, as if to add insult to injury. I closed my eyes. In one year at most I'd go walking with Charlotte down the Kurfürstendamm and we'd have our own little flat in Prenzlauer Berg, perhaps a little restaurant, a bar or a food stand. When I opened my eyes we were parking in front of Frau Hohenembs's house, in the very spot where there was never a free parking space, no matter what time of day or night. The fake police officers let me get out, then took my arms again. We climbed the steps, the woman rang the bell and Ida opened the door, holding an unopened tin of Russian caviar in her other hand. Her round face beamed. She's back! We've missed her so much! The dog leaped up at me. Putting his front paws around my neck, he was about to lick my face, which I tried to prevent by pushing his head down with both hands. It was the first time that he hadn't tried to thrust his muzzle between my legs straight away. From the drawing room I could hear the parrots say, She's back, she's back, not squawking as usual but with almost melodious voices, as if they'd swallowed chalk. Frau Hohenembs pushed Ida to one side and thanked the police officers. I'm very sorry she's caused you so much trouble. She does run away sometimes, but she's never got that far before. She almost escaped over the border! She threatened me with her index finger, then raised her shoulders ruefully. The man made a slight bow and tapped a finger on his cap. No big deal for us, these sorts of things happen almost every day, just keep a more watchful eye on her in future. Ha, you don't need to tell me that; she's always trying to outsmart us, our little runaway. She giggled with her hand in front of her mouth. It's hard to understand, the man said. You'd think anyone would feel happy in a house like this. But people are never satisfied with what they've got. We see all sorts of things, Frau Hohenembs, believe you me. What a drama! And all because of me. I tried to run away, but Ida held tightly onto my arm like a vice, whispering into my ear, Don't be stupid, that won't get you anywhere, make the best of it. The dog put his tall body in my way and leaned his warmth against my belly. The fake policeman turned around briefly and smiled, then the two of them were gone and Ida closed the door.

*

When she no longer wanted to take me on her travels, engaging a younger woman in my place, I was deeply upset. For her I was not fast and strong enough any more. I could barely keep up on the long hikes, I had never coped well with the sea voyages and the permanent change of climate disagreed with me. Her restlessness, into which she dragged me and all those around her, gradually undermined my health, but I would have put up with anything just for the chance to stay near to her. She wrote me the sweetest letters, full of longing and love. I often had to go without seeing her for months. It was sad to be replaced just like that.

*

Everything is as it was before. The silent breakfast, the meat juice, the Greek lessons, a silent lunch after the Greek teacher has slammed the door, endless hikes, errands, shopping, secretly emptying jars, the baron at the corner – he never mentioned the money again. I keep it in the same envelope he handed to me. The envelope is quite crumpled. Every night I count the money with my trembling hands and I stroke the smooth banknotes. There are fewer and fewer of them. Ida doesn't go to see the baron as much these days; she often has to lie down during the day as her legs swell up and she's got varicose veins that are wrapped around her calves and thighs like string. My suspicion is that she's diabetic, but she won't go to the doctor. Now I wear a housecoat with a diagonal stripe, which I take off when we eat. I have it in a variety of colour combinations. It's terribly practical. You slip it on and at once feel like you're well dressed. Frau Hohenembs also gave me a wide lilac velvet armband. It feels nice against the skin. As soon as it gets greasy I'm given a new one. Two weeks ago we had a very promising guest: a girl who is as thin as a British model. Frau Hohenembs invited her over for some Gugelhupf and the girl took the other half of it home with her.

Peirene

Contemporary
European Literature.
Thought provoking,
well designed, short.

*'Two-hour books to be
devoured in a single sitting:
literary cinema for those
fatigued by film.'* TLS

Subscribe

Peirene Press publishes series of world-class contemporary novellas. An annual subscription consists of three books chosen from across the world connected by a single theme.

The books will be sent out in December (in time for Christmas), May and September. Any title in the series already in print when you order will be posted immediately.

The perfect way for book lovers to collect all the Peirene titles.

'A class act.' GUARDIAN

'Two-hour books to be devoured in a single sitting: literary cinema for those fatigued by film.' TLS

£35   1 Year Subscription (3 books, free p&p)

£65   2 Year Subscription (6 books, free p&p)

£90   3 Year Subscription (9 books, free p&p)

Peirene Press, 17 Cheverton Road, London N19 3BB
T 020 7686 1941
E subscriptions@peirenepress.com

www.peirenepress.com/shop
with secure online ordering facility

Peirene's Series

SMALL EPIC: UNRAVELLING SECRETS

NO 7
The Brothers by Asko Sahlberg
Translated from the Finnish by Emily Jeremiah and Fleur Jeremiah
'Intensely visual.' INDEPENDENT ON SUNDAY

NO 8
The Murder of Halland by Pia Juul
Translated from the Danish by Martin Aitken
'A brilliantly drawn character.' TLS

NO 9
Sea of Ink by Richard Weihe
Translated from the Swiss German by Jamie Bulloch
'Delicate and moving.' INDEPENDENT

....

TURNING POINT:
REVOLUTIONARY MOMENTS

NO 10
The Mussel Feast by Birgit Vanderbeke
Translated from the German by Jamie Bulloch
'An extraordinary book.' STANDPOINT

NO 11
Mr Darwin's Gardener by Kristina Carlson
Translated from the Finnish by Emily Jeremiah and Fleur Jeremiah
'Something miraculous.' GUARDIAN

NO 12
Chasing the King of Hearts by Hanna Krall
Translated from the Polish by Philip Boehm
'A remarkable find.' SUNDAY TIMES

COMING-OF-AGE: TOWARDS IDENTITY

NO 13
The Dead Lake by Hamid Ismailov
Translated from the Russian by Andrew Bromfield
'Immense poetic power.' GUARDIAN

NO 14
The Blue Room by Hanne Ørstavik
Translated from the Norwegian by Deborah Dawkin
'Shrewd and psychologically adroit.' LANCASHIRE
EVENING POST

NO 15
Under the Tripoli Sky by Kamal Ben Hameda
Translated from the French by Adriana Hunter
'It is excellent.' SUNDAY TIMES

....

CHANCE ENCOUNTER: MEETING THE OTHER

NO 16
White Hunger by Aki Ollikainen
Translated from the Finnish by Emily Jeremiah and Fleur Jeremiah
'A tale of epic substance.'
LOS ANGELES REVIEW OF BOOKS

NO 17
Reader for Hire by Raymond Jean
Translated from the French by Adriana Hunter
'A book that will make you want to read more books.'
COSMOPOLITAN

NO 18
The Looking-Glass Sisters by Gøhril Gabrielsen
Translated from the Norwegian by John Irons
'Disturbs and challenges.' THE NATIONAL

COUNTERPOINTS ARTS

Peirene Press is proud to support Counterpoints Arts.

Counterpoints Arts is a charity that promotes the creative arts by and about refugees and migrants in the UK.

'We are living in a time of human displacement. We need bold and imaginative interventions to help us make sense of migration. And who better to do this than artists who are engaging with this issue.'

ALMIR KOLDZIC AND ÁINE O'BRIEN, DIRECTORS, COUNTERPOINTS ARTS

By buying this book you are helping Counterpoints Arts enhance the cultural integration of refugees – a mission which will surely change our society for the better.

Peirene will donate 50p from the sale of this book to the charity.

www.counterpointsarts.org.uk